"I haven't brought
anyone else here."

"Does that answer the question I saw
in your eyes?" Zeb said, his tone
mocking her. "I have a perfectly
adequate flat in London for the
purposes you're thinking of. I come
here when I want peace and quiet."

Seeing the tired look in his eyes,
Aldona realized that a man who ruled
the massive company Zeb did must
indeed need a place to go where no
one could easily reach him.

"No one's likely to find you here,
then?" she asked shyly.

"No. But then we don't want to be
disturbed, do we?" he replied
sardonically.

Color flooded Aldona's face, and she
moved away from him into the
sitting room.

"Blushes?" he queried. "What sort of
thoughts are raging through your
sweet mind, Aldona?"

JESSICA STEELE

price to be met

Harlequin Books

TORONTO • NEW YORK • LOS ANGELES • LONDON
AMSTERDAM • PARIS • SYDNEY • HAMBURG
STOCKHOLM • ATHENS • TOKYO • MILAN

Harlequin Presents first edition May 1983
ISBN 0-373-10596-7

Original hardcover edition published in 1980
by Mills & Boon Limited

CHAPTER ONE

MAKING her way to the house where her father lived, the house where she too had lived until six months ago when he had remarried, Aldona sent up a prayer that this Wednesday wouldn't find Lionel Downs in her father's sitting room.

She was heedless that the early September evening had turned chilly, her mind full of the best way to tell her father that her brief engagement to Guy Stinton was off. She knew he liked Guy and approved of their engagement. It had been through him she had met Guy. Had met Lionel Downs too, she recalled without pleasure.

The three men all worked at Sebastian Thackeray Limited, a company that specialised in digital electronics. Roland Mayhew, her father, had only started there six months ago; Aldona preferred not to dwell on the fifteen-month period of unemployment he had lived through after his redundancy from his previous firm, though something good had come from those days when he had fretted about being out of a job and the bleak prospect facing him that at fifty-six, coupled with his suspect heart, no one was going to take him on. For it had been during one of his afternoon walks, exercise in moderation being good for him, the doctors said, that he had met Barbara, off work having attended the funeral of a cousin that day and sitting on a bench in a nearby park.

It seemed to Aldona, as she neared the house she had grown up in, that her father's fortunes had taken an upswing from that moment on, for shortly after meeting Barbara he had found himself a job in the accounting department of Sebastian Thackeray Limited, a job he could do standing on his head, and working in close liaison with the firm's internal auditor, Lionel Downs.

Guy Stinton worked in the accounts department too, and it had been on one of her regular Wednesday evening visits to her old home that Aldona had met Guy, who had called to borrow one of her father's books on mathematics.

She arrived at the front door, and paused, feeling slightly awkward in not knowing whether to use her latch key or ring and wait. Always very close to her father, she had watched him like a hawk after his heart attack three years ago, but had found herself a small flat and moved out when he had married. Barbara was mistress here now.

Aldona still wasn't sure whether she liked Barbara or not, though she was fair-minded enough to consider that having been so close to her parent she might have a touch of resentment in her feelings for her father's bride. It had been that fear that she might unwittingly show resentment when Barbara had come to take her place that had decided her to move out. Her father's medical consultant had told her three years ago that he could lead a more or less normal life, and would live his natural span provided he didn't do anything silly, but most importantly, the consultant had underlined, his life must be lived without stress. Stress, it had been impressed upon her, could bring on another heart attack.

Conscious she had been dithering on the door step for far too long, Aldona inserted her key in the door and pushed it inwards, to close it and turn and see her fair, curly-haired stepmother, looking five years younger than her forty-two years, coming down the stairs, a badminton racquet in her hand.

The greeting that hovered on Aldona's lips vanished as

she stared at Barbara in surprise. It wasn't that Barbara seemed to have grown younger since her marriage, or the fact that she was obviously on her way out to play badminton, a sport she excelled at but which her husband could not join in, but the fact her sports gear was topped by a magnificent fur coat Aldona had never known she had possessed.

'Your father's upstairs.' Barbara was the first to speak, her tone, Aldona thought, a shade aloof, though it could be that she felt the same strain she herself was feeling that the one man they both loved more than any other was upstairs, and he appeared to be the only thing they had in common. Then Barbara seemed to notice her eyes were on her fabulous fur, and said, a trifle selfconsciously, Aldona thought, 'I know a mink coat is a mite ostentatious to go to badminton in, but I've only just got it and I couldn't resist wearing it.'

'It's very nice,' said Aldona, an understatement, wanting to say it was beautiful, but finding it difficult to be natural.

'Would you like to wait for your father in the sitting room?' Barbara offered. 'I'm sorry I can't wait with you, but I'm late as it is.'

Aldona moved away from the front door, feeling an awkwardness she didn't care for. There had been no time for her to get to know Barbara, since her father's courtship of her had been of a brief duration, and with Wednesday being Barbara's badminton night, they were still virtually strangers to each other.

'Have a good game,' she wished her, and as Barbara went out, she crossed the hall to the sitting room.

Since she had thought she would be over the difficulty she had found in speaking to Barbara by the time her father came down, her spirits dropped to see she was not the sole occupant of the sitting room. Her heart fell to her feet as she recognised the bulky, flaccid-featured Lionel Downs as he got out of his chair, cigar in one hand and a glass of Scotch in the other, and stood, his concupiscent gaze, to her mind, mentally stripping her.

'Hello, Aldona,' he greeted her, not moving any nearer but standing where he was as though satisfied he could get a better view of her slender but curvaceous figure from there. 'This is a pleasure.'

'I didn't see your car outside,' she said, knowing that since he was a friend of her father's she had to hide the revulsion she felt for this shifty-eyed man.

'There wasn't room to park outside, and since Barbara usually takes her car out on a Wednesday, I thought better than to block her way by parking on the drive.'

Very thoughtful of him, she was sure, she thought, hoping her father would appear before too long. 'My father's upstairs, Barbara tells me,' she said, purely for something to say. Here was someone else she had very little in common with either.

'He left me to go and kiss his wife goodbye. He wants to go carefully,' Lionel added, his voice loaded with suggestion. 'Too much of the wrong sort of exercise with his heart condition might not be good for him.'

How could her father be friends with this type of man? He sickened her to her stomach. 'My father has recovered from his illness,' she told him, keeping her temper in check, but unable to do anything about the cutting tone in her voice. 'It's three years now since he had any trouble.'

At her tone, Lionel Downs dropped his suggestive bantering and told her bluntly, 'Well, he wasn't looking too bright when he went to say cheerio to Barbara. And the length of time he's been away is a good indication that he's taking time off to take one of his heart pills.'

Heart pills! Aldona felt fear strike at the gut of her. Her father was on regular medication, but he also had a supply of emergency tablets. As far as she knew he had never had to take one of the fast-acting emergency pills, but ... She was at the door on her way to race upstairs when Lionel Downs said quickly:

'For goodness' sake don't panic. You know he hates fuss. He wasn't looking all that bad.'

'But you said ...' she began, halting her steps as realisation came that her father was likely to get upset if she went charging upstairs and started questioning him about his health. He was a proud man, and it offended him to have to admit to being ill. He had been cross with her on more than one occasion in the past, accusing her of trying to wrap him up in cotton wool.

'Perhaps I overstated the case,' her father's superior at work but nowhere else, said. 'It's just that ...' He broke off, obviously not intending to say any more. But Aldona wasn't prepared to leave it there.

'It's just that what?' she asked sharply, turning to face him with a purposeful look in her anxious brown eyes that demanded an answer.

'Well, I know he's very worried ...'

'Worried?' she picked up before he could continue. Fear for her father had her by the throat, and there was no sign about her then of the girl who had just tried to cut him down to size. 'What's he worrying over?' she asked urgently, ignoring that Lionel's eyes lingered too long over her curves, his lips moving almost as if he could taste her. Agitation was getting the better of her. It was the first priority that her father shouldn't worry, and if Lionel Downs didn't soon tell her what he so obviously knew, she felt disturbed enough to go and shake it out of him.

At last he spoke, and it was no help whatsoever to hear him say, 'He doesn't want you to know.'

Didn't want her to know! Her mind sought for what could possibly be worrying him. Since he had only been friends with Lionel Downs for a very short time then it must be something to do with work, for she couldn't see her father confiding to him his worries on so short an acquaintance. Oh no. he wasn't in danger of being made redundant again, was he? Oh, dear lord, say it wasn't that, it would just about kill his pride if that happened again. Common sense threaded its way in as she recalled reading that Thackerays, world leaders in their field, were going from strength to strength. No, it couldn't be redundancy. She pushed her panic behind her, and her voice was a shade arrogant as she said:

'I insist you tell me, Mr Downs.'

'You insist, do you?' he replied, letting her see she was going the wrong way about getting him to tell her anything. But fear for her father's health had her in its grip and she could do nothing to soften her attitude.

'Yes, I insist. My father shouldn't be allowed to worry—you must know that. So I would be obliged if you'll tell me what the trouble is, so I can help to sort it out.'

'You'd be wasting your time trying to sort this one out, girlie,' he told her, and she could see her tone had niggled him. 'Not unless you've got two thousand pounds salted away somewhere.'

'Two thousand pounds!' she gasped. He couldn't mean her father owed someone two thousand pounds! Barbara had given up her job on her marriage, so there was only one income coming in and she knew her father's savings had gone when he'd been out of work for so long. But two thousand pounds! He just couldn't be in debt for that amount.

'That's what it'll take to remove this load of worry.'

'But—but how? Why?'

'How?' he replied. 'Very cleverly, I would say. But not clever enough to deceive me.'

What was he talking about? Clever? Her father had a good brain, had worked in high finance before his illness, had then taken a less stressful job that had ended in redundancy, but it had been his cleverness with figures that had got him his present job over younger, fitter applicants. But what was this horrible man suggesting? That her father had been very clever, but not clever enough to deceive him? Her stomach turned over as she recalled Lionel Downs position with Thackerays was that of internal auditor.

'This is—something to do with Thackerays, isn't it?' she asked, feeling ice cold as she waited for his answer.

'Well, since you're guessing along the right lines,' he said, sounding pompous, 'I might just as well tell you that as chief auditor I discovered a discrepancy in the books.' His voice was not strong, but it thundered in her brain as he added, 'Two thousand pounds had gone missing.'

'Two thousand pounds,' Aldona repeated, and while knowing it was absolutely laughable to suspect that a man of her father's integrity should be responsible for its loss, she knew that was exactly what Lionel Downs was suggesting.

'That's the amount,' he confirmed, going on to tell her, 'The external auditors are due in on Monday,' then shatteringly, 'I'm giving your father every opportunity of recovering the money before they come in.'

Aldona groped for the nearest chair, knowing she would have to sit down before she fell down. He believed her

father had taken that money, that much was clear. But she
didn't believe it, couldn't believe it, thought she must
have misunderstood him in some way.

'You're saying,' she said, needing to have the words
said before they would sink in, 'that you believe my father
has st-stolen two thousand pounds from Sebastian
Thackeray Limited?'

Lionel Downs looked startled and she thought that
some of the brain power she had inherited from her father
had quickly summed up all that had been said, for after
that one quick surprised look he looked away from her
as though he was sorry she had learned such a terrible
thing from him. He has no need to feel sorry for me, she
thought; she knew her father better than he did, and he
just wouldn't do such a thing. What would he want with
two thousand pounds anyway? As she was about to defend
her father in no uncertain terms, suddenly, so swiftly it
almost took her breath, there came into her mind a picture
of Barbara coming down the stairs wearing that magnificent
fur. Oh no! she thought, wanting to dislodge the picture
as a groan escaped her. She knew her father was very
much in love with his new wife, but surely he hadn't
turned his back on the honour he prized so dearly as to . . .

It was unthinkable, but she just couldn't get it out of
her mind. 'What—what will happen if he can't find the
money?' she found herself asking. If there was any truth
at all in what Lionel was saying, and she still couldn't
believe it, then he was right in one thing; her father
wouldn't be able to bear that she knew. All her questions
had to be asked before he joined them.

'Sebastian Thackeray isn't the sort of man who will
countenance this sort of thing,' she was told flatly. 'There'll
be a prosecution for sure.'

Prosecution! Oh God, it would kill him. Shock had

her in its grip, shaking her faith, making the only thought in her head that of knowing she somehow had to find a way of stopping her father being prosecuted. She opened her mouth to say something, but no sound came out. Then making a tremendous effort, she found her voice. 'What if I went to see Mr Thackeray?' she whispered. 'Told him of my father's heart condition. What if I promised to pay the money back?' She was ready to promise anything just then.

'Can you pay the money back? You don't earn very much at your job, do you?'

Aldona fell silent. She loved her job as an assistant in a day nursery, but what she made there only just covered her monthly expenses.

'But if I went to see him, told him about my father's ...'

'You'd be wasting your time. Apart from the fact that he's out of the country at the moment, he hasn't got time to waste on appointments with daughters of his employees. He'd have even less time for you when he knows you're the—er—daughter of a man who's embezzled the company of two thousand pounds.'

That word 'embezzled' hit her like a shower of ice cold water. But she had no time to dwell on it, for the sound of a door closing upstairs told her her father would be down any moment. Lionel Downs heard the sound too, and said quickly:

'Don't let on that you know anything. The shame of you knowing would mortify him.'

She didn't answer. He was right, of course. Her father had brought her up single-handed when her mother had died. From the age of five he had instilled in her a knowledge of right and wrong. Her upbringing had been stricter than most of her friends, but she hadn't minded because with all the severity of her upbringing there had been love

in abundance. But that it had been he who should be the
one to fall on the wrong side of that line between right
and wrong was something he wouldn't want her to know
until every chance of righting that wrong had been ex-
plored.

It was as she remembered his patient guidance in her
formative years that Aldona knew suddenly she had been
very, very wrong to think that he had done what he stood
accused of. It just wasn't in him, and she felt bitterly
ashamed that her fears for his health had so overwhelmed
her that she had forgotten for even a moment what an upright man he was.

The door of the sitting room opened before she could
tell Lionel Downs that she just didn't believe a word he
said. Then Roland Mayhew was in the room, and she had
to stifle a gasp of horror that there was no resemblance in
this grey-faced, worried-looking man to the twinkling-eyed,
pink-cheeked man she had visited last week.

She recovered quickly, hiding as she had learned to do
since his heart attack any suggestion that she was concerned about him. 'Hello, Dad,' she said brightly, and it
was like having a door slammed in the face of her belief in
him when he didn't meet her eyes. Her father had never
been afraid to look anyone in the eye, but here he was
avoiding looking at her, his own daughter! Oh God, he
looks awful, she thought, wanting to rush over to him and
help him to a chair. But she knew she dared not. 'We
thought you'd got lost,' she said cheerfully, hoping he
wouldn't see she was forcing herself to sound lighthearted.
Though by the look of him, whether she was lighthearted
or not was the least of his troubles. Again he refused to
meet her eyes, and she knew then, with a lead weight in
her stomach, that he had done this dreadful thing.

'It's—er—started to rain,' he said, not looking at her.

'I've been fiddling with that window with the broken sash cord in your old room. I'll get it fixed one of these days.' His voice sounded lighthearted too, but Aldona saw him flash Lionel Downs an urgently questioning look as though asking what they had been talking about in his absence. 'I didn't hear you arrive,' he said as he passed her and went over to his favourite chair near to where Lionel Downs was standing. She gathered from that that had he known he would have been down much sooner rather than give the auditor at Thackerays a chance to tell her anything.

She watched as he came level with Lionel Downs. They were much the same height, though there any resemblance ended, for her father was white-haired as opposed to the other man's reddish-brown hair—she had thought on one occasion that he dyed it—and her father was lean to the point of being thin, where Lionel Downs was well covered. And it was as her father paused by his friend that any doubts she had been nursing that he just couldn't have done what had been said were decisively knocked on the head as she heard him say in an urgent undertone:

'She looks pale—you haven't told her about the money, have you?'

Her legs went like jelly on hearing the low-voiced reply. 'If it's to be prison, she'll be the last one to know.'

She had her back to them both when her father settled in his chair, and was admiring a framed tapestry picture that hadn't been hanging on the wall last Wednesday.

'This is gorgeous,' she said, composure coming from somewhere as she turned to face them. 'I haven't seen it before, have I?'

'It is nice, isn't it?' her father agreed. 'Barbara made it.'

Aldona spent about an hour with them. For the first time she was glad Lionel Downs was there too. On previous

Wednesdays she had spent a good deal of the time wishing he would go. But tonight his presence helped her to overcome the strain she was feeling. She knew her father was feeling the strain too, though she dared not give him anything to be suspicious over by going too early. At nine o'clock she stood to her feet.

'I'm on at seven-thirty in the morning, I'd better make tracks for my flat,' she told the two men, expecting Lionel Downs would stay behind, though hoping he wouldn't say anything to worry her parent any more than he was worried already.

'I'll give you a lift,' he surprised her by saying. And as the rain that had been pouring down steadily outside for the past hour lashed against the window, he gave her a charming smile and said, 'It's bucketing down out there, you'll get drenched.'

About to protest she could get a taxi, Aldona looked at her father, sensitive to his every thought. Would he be suspicious if she refused, wonder if she knew they had things to talk about that she wasn't to know about?

'I'd be glad of a lift, thank you, Mr Downs,' she said.

'Lionel,' he invited, then patted her shoulder in a way her father would think meant he thought of her as a little girl.

Her father came to the door with them. 'You'll come back for a nightcap when you've seen Aldona home?' he asked Lionel Downs.

'Start pouring it now, Roland,' Lionel Downs replied. 'I shouldn't be very long.'

Once in the car she abstractedly started to give directions to where she lived to the man who had volunteered to drive her, only to learn that he already knew.

'I asked your father the first time I met you,' he told her, the car already in motion, and as she sent him a startled look he turned to give her what might have been a comforting smile, only she couldn't tell in the dark, and added, which didn't comfort her at all, 'I took a shine to you from the very beginning, Aldona.'

'Er——' she began, searching for something to say that wouldn't offend him in the circumstances, since by not reporting her father straightaway he had proved what a good friend he was, but wanting to kill anything else he might have to say. 'That's—er—very kind of you,' she managed at last, feeling sick and hypocritical and wishing she'd called a taxi after all.

'I've liked you from the very beginning,' he told her, and not receiving a rebuff patted her knee, making her want to flatten herself against the door away from him.

He removed his hand and she breathed more easily, staring stonily straight in front of her. Her mind went back to the worn and tired-looking man they had just left. Lionel Downs had mentioned the word 'prison' and she had to swallow down tears at just the very thought. Her father would be dead before it got that far, she knew it as well as she knew that night followed day.

'Have you given Master Guy the old heave-ho? I noticed you aren't wearing your engagement ring,' said the man beside her, showing he had been far more observant than her father. But that wasn't surprising; her father had far more important things on his mind than to notice the absence of her ring.

'I'm no longer engaged,' she said, then urgently, 'Don't tell my father when you go back, will you? I don't want him to have anything else to worry about, and with Guy on holiday until Monday,' her voice faded as she added, 'he needn't know until then.' And on Monday the outside auditors would be in, and the fact that she had broken her engagement to Guy would hardly bother her father at all.

The car drew up outside the house where she had her

flat, and in desperation she turned to the man who was being such a good friend to her father.

'Mr Downs—Lionel, can't anything be done to—to stop the auditors from finding out? I mean, couldn't you...' She couldn't go on. The firmly entrenched standards of her upbringing, the deep-rooted, thick line between right and wrong was at war within her that here she was ready to beg this man to break his code of professional conduct and try to cover up what her father had done.

'I'm sorry, my dear,' he said, and sounded so deeply sorry that she warmed to him on her father's behalf. 'The only way to save Roland's neck is for that two thousand pounds to be paid into the bank by Monday.'

Numbly her hand groped for the handle of the car door, and she was on the point of opening it, her thoughts all with her father and far away from his friend, when his voice broke into the misery of her thoughts.

'I wonder, Aldona, how far you're prepared to go to help your father?'

Her hand left the door handle, and she turned to face him, words falling from her without the need to think about them. 'There's nothing I wouldn't do for him,' she said warmly, and it was true, though she hadn't thought the question necessary.

'In that case,' came the equally warm response, 'I think there may be a way ...'

'What? What? Tell me what it is?' Her words fell rapidly, hope surging in her breast. 'I'll do anything, anything in the world just so long as my father isn't prosecuted!'

Impatient for him to tell her the way he had thought of in which her father could be saved, it seemed long agonising minutes before he told her what he had in mind. And when he did, Aldona was hard put to it not to vomit on the spot. How she held down the revulsion in her stomach, she just didn't know. But she was too shaken for what seemed minutes afterwards to answer Lionel at all when he said:

'I'm going on holiday to Malta on Saturday. Come with me, Aldona, and I'll tonight give your father my personal post-dated cheque so that he can pay it into the firm's account first thing on Monday.'

Incredulously, her stomach threatening to give her away if she couldn't control it, she just stared at him. 'You mean ...' she gasped hoarsely at last, her mind not wanting to believe what her brain was telling her, 'you'll pay the two thousand pounds that will make my father's books balance if I come on holiday with you?' and because she just had to have it all settled now, because she just couldn't believe what her brain was telling her, 'if I come on holiday with you as—your—friend?'

'For two thousand quid, I'd want you to be more than just *a friend*,' he told her, and at her unmistakable gasp of horror, he added bluntly, 'You've been engaged, girlie —you know the score.'

Aldona knew then she was going to be sick, and she grabbed for the door handle, had the door open, and was gulping great breaths of the damp air outside when Lionel's voice floated after her, 'Give me a ring at the office tomorrow, girlie. You'll not get a better offer.'

She made it to the bathroom on the landing of the first floor, and retched till she could retch no more, then after leaving the bathroom tidy for the next person, her mind fighting off the hundred and one thoughts that bombarded her, with tears streaming down her face, she slowly made her way to the top of the house and her attic flat.

And there all other thoughts were tossed aside as she collapsed into a chair and allowed herself to dwell on the

only two points that had to be considered. One, that her
father was in serious trouble, the disclosure of which
could bring on a heart attack which could kill him, if the
pressure of worry didn't kill him first. The other point
being that with Lionel Downs having 'taken a shine' to her
as he put it, the genuine love and concern she had for her
father was being put to a very real test.

A picture of the heavily built, shifty-eyed Lionel Downs
came into her mind and with it the way he had of mentally
undressing her every time he looked at her, and she shud-
dered and knew she would be sick again if she allowed
herself to dwell on that picture. Instead she forced herself to think only of her father, of the stress he was under
when his doctor had said stress must be avoided at all
costs.

Lionel Downs would be back with him by now—if he
was such a friend, wouldn't he have offered to loan him
the two thousand without strings since he didn't appear
to be short of funds to have made the suggestion he had
made to her—she mustn't think about him. She must
think only of her father. Her father, who would spend
another stressful night nursing his worries—— Yet she
had the power to give him peace from his worries—and
tonight.

Without being aware she had made a decision, Aldona
picked up her purse and went to the pay phone that had
been installed on the ground floor for use of the tenants.
She paused before dialling her father's number, getting
what she had to say fixed firmly in her mind. Then, with
icy cold fingers, she dialled.

Her father answered the phone, and his voice had a
forced note of jocularity in it as on hearing her voice, he
asked what she had left behind this time.

'You'd never believe it,' she laughed, her laughter sounding sick in her own ears, though she thought he would have too much on his mind to notice it, 'but I can't find my key to the junior aspirin cupboard at the nursery. Do you think Mr Downs would mind checking the floor of his car, it may have dropped out of my bag when I was getting my door key out.'

She waited what seemed an age as her father passed on her message. Then as she had hoped, it was Lionel Downs who came on the phone after his fruitless search, and she was sure when he said briefly, 'No key,' that he had rumbled that it was only an excuse to get him to the phone. But just hearing his voice sent shivers of distaste along her spine. Oh Dad, I can't, she thought, then saw his face as it had been the last time she had seen it.

'W-would you give that cheque to my father tonight?' she asked, and didn't have to add any more as the answer came back:

'With pleasure, Aldona.'

When she got up the next morning she was forcibly re-minding herself of some of the thoughts that had gone through her head through that wakeful night. She was twenty-four, and although Lionel Downs had been wide off the mark with the implication behind his, 'You've been engaged, girlie—you know the score,' there were, she knew, plenty of girls who went away on the kind of holiday he had proposed. That the ratio of girls who went away with men of his age, and she thought he was nearer sixty than fifty, was far fewer than girls who selected men nearer their own age group just didn't have to be thought about.

Automatically she washed and dressed and made her way to the nursery in the poorer part of London. The work she did was very often exhausting, and feeling exhausted before she got started she welcomed the day where the children's

constant needs would, she hoped, leave her little time for
thoughts that were taking on nightmare proportions.

Expecting to be fully occupied that morning, whether it
was because she was giving the lead by being quiet herself, miraculously the toddlers in her care seemed to be
being impeccably behaved. It couldn't last, she knew that,
and as she saw each one occupied without tears, her mind
couldn't escape her own problems.

In the cold light of day, last night's happenings seemed
unbelievable. Yet she knew everything that had gone
on had happened. She *had* made that terrible discovery
about her father. She *had* agreed to go away with Lionel
Downs. And, oh, God, she prayed, there must be some
other way out.

At eleven o'clock she went into the office, found it
empty, and dialled her father's number with the idea
growing in her that somehow she must get Barbara to
sell her fur coat. But as Barbara's cool tones gave her
number, she came up against the brick wall of the lack
of friendship between the two of them, and she just
couldn't even hint that her father was in trouble, that he
had paid for that coat with money that wasn't his. If he
loved Barbara so much that he could steal for her, she
realised suddenly, he would never forgive her if because
of anything she said Barbara walked out on him if she
found out what he had done.

'Hello, Barbara, it's me, Aldona,' she said when seconds
had ticked by and Barbara had repeated her number a
second time. 'Er—I was wondering if my father was all
right? I—er—thought he wasn't looking too well last
night.' She was aware she wasn't being very tactful and
was doing nothing to further any friendship between her
and her stepmother by implying that Roland Mayhew
wasn't looking so well now that she wasn't looking after

him. But she was at a loss to give any other excuse for her call.

And then Barbara was replying without any of the hostility she had thought would be coming her way. 'I thought the same myself,' she agreed. 'I thought he had something on his mind,' then she was confiding, 'To tell you the truth, I was so worried about him I said I wouldn't go to play badminton last night. But you know how he hates being fussed over, and when he insisted I went, I thought since he'd told me what a splendid job you did in looking after him after his illness, that you'd keep an eye on him while I was out. But you've no need to worry about him, Aldona,' she added, a lightness entering her voice. 'I played a rotten game because he was so much on my mind, but when I came home there he was sitting knocking back the Scotch with Lionel Downs, looking a better colour and as though he hadn't a care in the world. He was actually singing in the bathroom this morning, for all we had such a downpour last night.'

Aldona came away from the phone, the weight that was dragging her down temporarily forgotten, Barbara's words still with her, her reference to her father's singing voice that could make it rain, and the forthcoming attitude Barbara had shown when relieving her of concern for her father.

It was obvious to her then that Lionel Downs must have given him the post-dated cheque he had spoken of, probably had excused it having to be post-dated by saying he had to arrange the transfer of such an amount into his current account at the bank. The heavy burden had been lifted from her father's shoulders, thank God. It was now up to her with her sound heart to take that stress.

After lunch was over and the children settled for their afternoon nap, she went looking for Mrs Armstrong, the

woman in charge of the nursery, and explained that something had come up and she needed her two weeks' leave
as from Saturday.

Mrs Armstrong was a plump, motherly sort of woman,
but a lady who had been known to take to task anyone
who wasn't pulling their weight. But she liked Aldona,
and privately thought they were lucky to have such a gem
who seemed to have a natural knack of dealing with the
most unruly of children; and it had to be said that their
angelic expressions far belied the little demon that lurked
inside them when they had a touch of the 'I won'ts'. It was
on such occasions that Aldona was always sent for if she
was in the building. So although they were constantly
short-staffed, not many putting up with the small salaries
and the hard work involved, she looked at Aldona, saw
the look of strain about her, noticed the poor girl looked
as though she hadn't slept all night, and then as Aldona
nervously pushed her left hand down the side of her
white overall, she noticed the absence of her engagement
ring.

'You really need the next two weeks off, Aldona?' she
asked. 'I don't need to tell you we're short-handed, with
Wendy off with a summer cold.'

'I really need the time off,' Aldona said, hoping Wendy
would be fit by Monday, but knowing she would have to
have the time off with or without permission.

'Very well,' said Mrs Armstrong. 'I expect we'll muddle
through somehow.'

As expected, the children's exemplary behaviour hadn't
lasted, and after trying to get through to young Elton
Smith that it wasn't polite to try and push a crayon up
little Olivia Reading's nose, and dealing with Olivia's tears,
Aldona eventually left work twenty minutes late at ten
to four, knowing that as soon as she got home she was

going to have to ring Lionel Downs to find out the
arrangements for Saturday.

With a feeling of getting it over and done with now,
she didn't bother with going up to her flat first, but
stopped at the ground floor and rang the offices of Sebastian
Thackeray Limited and was soon hearing the voice that
was beginning to make her flesh creep as she listened to
him telling her he would call for her on Saturday, sicken-
ing innuendo in every sentence, telling her to make sure
she brought her passport, and that they were in for a great
time. Several times she had to resist the urge to slam the
phone back on the hook. Then she thought to ask the
question that had come to her last night, had bothered
her all day, and would have her slamming the phone down
yet if she got the wrong answer, though how she was going
to save her father if the answer she got was in the positive.

'Just one more thing,' she said, finding it impossible to
tack his name on the end. 'My father has never discussed
you with me, so I don't know, but—you're not married, are
you?'

At that point she wasn't anywhere near sure what she
wanted his answer to be, but if it was, 'Yes, I am,' she
knew her passport was going to stay exactly where it was
in her drawer. She knew he was enjoying keeping her waiting for his reply, and then it came, accompanied by a
scoffing laugh.

'Of course I'm not. What do you take me for?'

Aldona didn't tell him. Quietly she replaced the receiver.

CHAPTER TWO

THE flight to Malta had taken just over three hours, but to a highly tensed Aldona it had seemed like thirty. She had spent most of yesterday in coming to terms with herself, of reminding herself over and over again as panic repeatedly hit her that she was doing this for her father. And at last, by telling herself if she didn't go through with it then the end result could be that she was responsible for her father's death, she had packed her case. It was a sobering thought, a thought that had her knowing that of the two choices she had to live with afterwards, she could better live with the thought that she had been the paid— plaything—of a man on the way to being old enough to be her grandfather, than the unbearable thought of having ignored the chance of saving her father from going to an early grave.

The hotel Lionel Downs had selected was modern, but smaller than some they had passed, and she waited some yards away from him as he went to check them in, trying to dissociate herself from him while knowing that when he turned she would have to join him, and since she was sure he had reserved only one room, then everyone would know the exact extent of their relationship.

He turned. 'Come on, sweetie,' he said, his shifty eyes going over her with that look that brought a flare of pink colour to her normally pale olive complexion, especially as she noticed the receptionist's eyes were on her.

Silently she went with him, a hotel porter leading the way from the lift and escorting them to a light airy room, the first thing noticeable, to Aldona at any rate, was that

26

it had twin beds. Looking for pluses, there being far too many minuses, she took heart that at least when she went to sleep she wouldn't have to share a bed with Lionel. While he dealt with the porter, she went and examined the bathroom, ticked up another plus that it had a sturdy bolt on the other side of the door, then turned back into the room to see the porter had gone and she was alone with the man who was fast turning her stomach each time she looked at him.

He was eyeing her now, the fact that this time his look wasn't stripping her letting her know he was angry with her about something. He didn't take very long to acquaint her with the reason for his anger.

'You're going to have to drop that touch-me-not attitude if our holiday is going to be a success,' he said abruptly.

'Touch-me-not attitude?' she hedged, knowing full well what he was talking about, but making believe she didn't.

'I'm just about sick and tired of you flinching from me every time I go to touch you.' The fact that she'd, casually she thought, moved her hand out of reach every time his podgy hand had come near hers on the plane hadn't gone unnoticed, then. 'Nobody dragged you here,' he went on, his face growing red in his anger, and doing nothing to enhance his looks. 'You came with me of your own free will, and I paid dearly for you. So just you drop your hoity-toity airs and graces and remember you're here with me, and start looking as though you're glad of the fact and not as though you'd like to stick your nose in the air and pretend you don't know me.'

Aldona couldn't in all fairness answer anything to that. As he had said, he had paid for her. She couldn't even say she hadn't come here of her own free will, because the choice had been hers. She hadn't known she had come across as 'hoity-toity', but feeling so cold towards him,

no warmth in her at all for him, that could be the way she
struck him, she supposed.

'I'm s-sorry,' she found herself apologising, and rather
than tell him that the thought of him touching her was
threatening to make her go under, she excused herself by
saying, 'I have been a bit on edge, I admit, but I've been
anxious in case my father found out what I was doing.'

For a moment she wondered if she had said the wrong
thing, for he seemed so touchy and could easily feel
offended if he gathered from that that her father would
have a fit if he knew she had come away with his senior.
But apparently he didn't want her father to know either,
at least he showed no offence at her remark.

'Well, he won't find out from me,' he said, his red
colour fading as he came over and placed one heavy arm
around her shoulders.

Oh, she thought, her senses screaming in alarm, he's
not going to start anything now, is he? She had to force
herself to stand stock still when what she wanted to do was
to go racing from the room.

'Er—shall I unpack for you?' she plucked out of the
air, the feel of his arm heavy around her shoulders making
her brain seize up.

The arm dropped away, but she didn't dare move, and
like a frozen statue she heard him say as he moved away,
'You do that. I'm going to find myself a drink.'

The minute the door had closed behind him, she sank
down on the bed nearest to her, one hand going to her
mouth, the other to her stomach. Oh, this was awful, she
thought in despair, and got up to begin feverishly to unpack, knowing if she didn't get busy keeping herself
occupied, she would end up a nervous wreck.

She tackled her own unpacking first, feeling distaste at
having volunteered to unpack Lionel's personal belongings.
Only by shutting her mind off was she able to tackle his

suitcases. Then, feeling stifled, she changed into light-weight slacks and a shirt and left the room.

As though they contained the plague she avoided any of the hotel's bars and hurried outside, only slowing her pace when her feet met sand, then she picked her way across the hotel's small but private beach, making for the only isolated spot where sand was met by limestone rocks.

She sat down, drawing her knees up and looping her arms around them, her shoulder-length black hair sheltering her nape from the sun as she bent her head forward and let her mind drift.

Her father had been surprised when she had telephoned him last night to say she wouldn't be seeing him for the next couple of Wednesdays as she was taking two weeks of her annual holiday to go and stay with Hilary. Hilary was an old school friend, known and approved of by him. Hilary had been married now for a couple of years and was now the proud mother of a new baby Aldona had not yet seen.

'You're—er—quite happy?' her father had asked, and she had wondered at the question, until she realised he would think it odd she hadn't mentioned Guy.

'On top of the world,' she had answered brightly, knowing then that if she told him she was no longer engaged, he would start to worry and think she was going nursing a wounded heart. In all probability he was still worried about the auditors coming in next week just in case anything was discovered, so she didn't want to add to his worries by telling him at this stage that Guy wasn't her fiancé any longer. Though Guy could tell him on Monday, she supposed, but she'd learnt enough of Guy in the short time she had known him to know he was secretive about his personal affairs and would never volunteer any information unless pressed.

It was odd, she thought; Guy had come into her life

briefly, excited her with his surface charm, but she had never ever got beneath the surface of him. He had been good fun, but possessive. But she had truly thought herself in love with him, hadn't realised it was just his surface charm she had been infatuated with until that possessive streak in him had made her take a long-distance view of their relationship. Physically she had found him attractive, and had wondered at herself on more than one occasion that something inside her had prevented her from making that total commitment he had wanted. It had peeved him that she wouldn't go to bed with him, he'd tried to make her feel mean that she wouldn't. But there was just this something inside her, probably her strict upbringing, she didn't know, but she just couldn't step over that hard line drawn by her father. Oh, if her father could see her now, she thought, and lifted her head to look out to sea, not wanting thoughts of Lionel Downs to reach her.

Deliberately she switched her mind to that last meeting with Guy. She had thought he had accepted that because he had arranged to have a week off at short notice, it just wasn't possible for her to do the same. That she had done so now, she didn't want to think about. But that Tuesday evening Guy had urged her not to go into work for the rest of the week, and had turned resentful when she had told him they were short-handed at the nursery and she just couldn't not go in. Then before she had known what was happening they were in the middle of a row, with Guy saying he didn't know why she was wasting her time doing a job that paid only coppers when she was a fully trained secretary. It became clear from then on that he didn't think much of the job she did, and she regretted having told him of the work she had done previously. She had liked being a secretary, but after her father's illness the hours weren't suited to looking after the house and making sure he was properly looked after. She considered herself lucky to be taken on part time at the nursery since she had no training for that sort of work.

She could have gone back to being a secretary when he had married Barbara had she wanted to, but she hadn't wanted to. She loved her job. Mrs Armstrong had snatched at her offer when she had told her she was now available for full-time work. She resented Guy talking about the children as he had, as children who were born delinquents.

'No, they're not,' she had stoutly defended them. But he had looked frankly disbelieving and told her, since he couldn't get her to change her mind about taking the next three days off then she must love her job more than she loved him.

It was a form of blackmail and she knew it. But instead of reasoning with him, of trying to get him to see her point of view, thoroughly fed up with the whole argument, she had stared at his handsome, good-looking face, and thought, he's right, I do love my job more than I love him. And she had known at precisely that moment that she didn't want to marry him.

Her face went into solemn lines as she wondered if, had she been doing a higher paid job, she would have managed to save enough to pay the two thousand pounds without the need to sell herself. She shrugged the thought away. No point in wondering about ifs. If her father hadn't had that heart attack she wouldn't be here now. If he hadn't been made redundant he wouldn't be working for Sebastian Thackeray Limited, wouldn't have drawn out all his savings, wouldn't have had to sell the car. He had insisted her savings weren't to be touched and had never known with prices going up every week, or so it seemed, that most of her savings had gone to supplement the housekeeping money. It would have hurt his pride to know that. The rest of her savings she had drawn out and brought with her here. Why she had done that she wasn't sure, probably suffering from the same sense of pride that dogged her father. The pride that subconsciously said, Okay, so you've had to accept two thousand pounds from Lionel Downs, but he's not paying for anything you might need while you're here.

'Why so glum?'

The deep, well modulated voice startled her, bringing her head up to look a long way to the tall, fair-headed, fit-looking man who had come to stand a yard away from her and was now studying her wide brown eyes, straight delicate nose and warm, beautifully proportioned mouth. He was dressed as casually as she, in lightweight trousers and sports shirt. She didn't answer, and he spoke again, turning his head slightly and looking back the way he had come.

'What are you doing sitting over here by yourself? It's all happening over there.'

She didn't need to look to know he was referring to the other holiday makers making the most of enjoying themselves.

'I prefer my own company,' she said, and looked past him out to sea. If he couldn't take the hint that his company wasn't wanted, then he was less intelligent than his high forehead proclaimed.

'So do I,' he said, not a bit abashed, and to her amazement promptly selected the spot next to her and sat down.

Aldona continued to look out to sea, intent on ignoring him. Perhaps he'd take the hint and go away. She didn't want to get friendly with anyone staying in the hotel. Didn't want anyone sending her speculative glances when they saw her in company with Lionel Downs. And she had

to school herself to go against her nature, to be unfriendly
to this man who was impervious to her broad hint, because a part of her had recognised that although strictly
speaking he was not good-looking as Guy was, there was
something about him that was undeniably attractive. She
didn't need to look at him again to know he had a strong
dependable face, firm chin, an arrogant sort of nose—or
was that just the way he'd had to look down it to speak
to her from his height?

'Sensible girl to keep yourself covered up, seeing this is
your first day,' he said to the side of her.

'How did you . . .' The exclamation broke from her before she had time to reason that her lack of tan would have
told him that. 'I suppose I am a Persil shade of white,' she
answered her own half-asked question, and found herself
staring into deeply grey eyes that were openly admiring
her features. She turned her head to look out to sea again,
feeling an unaccountable knocking near her ribs. She
forced common sense in and told herself, how ridiculous!
One's heart didn't begin to hammer purely from looking
into deeply grey eyes.

'How long are you staying?' he enquired casually,
causing her to wonder if this was the first day of his holiday too and if he was making the first overtures for a little
holiday dalliance for the rest of his stay. Though her second
look at him, his unspoken reference to the rays of the sun,
had her noticing that he was already tanned to a very
becoming bronze.

'Two weeks,' she replied, keeping her voice cool, for any
ideas he might have could be allowed to go no further,
though what made her tack on, 'How long are you here
for?' she didn't know.

'I've booked in for tonight only,' he told her, and it
could have been her imagination, but she could have

sworn there was a hard note in his voice as he said it. As if his stay was something he hadn't looked forward to and had no intention of enjoying.

His answer firmly knocked on the head any idea she might have gained that he was trying his hand at a little light flirtation with her, for all the admiration she had seen in his eyes. Guy had told her she was beautiful, but he hadn't been the first to do so. She had seen admiration in other men's eyes for her before, but she felt a little let down this time by knowing this man's look had been one of mere passing appreciation.

'You're here on business?' she asked, thinking that must be the case since he was here for only one night, and relaxing somewhat that even if he did see her with her escort tonight then he wouldn't be here to give her a knowing look tomorrow.

'Something like that,' he said shortly, then changing the subject, 'What's your name?'

He was being anything but flirtatious now, and she realised she had mistaken he was trying to pick her up. It was purely as he had stated. He too liked his own company, and she was occupying the only spot on the private beach that was anyway near away from the crowd.

'Aldona Mayhew,' she told him, seeing no reason why she shouldn't since he wasn't likely to be looking her up. She turned again to look at him, but he was looking out to sea. 'What's yours?' she asked, feeling irked that he could take a couple of glances at her and promptly appear to forget her.

His glance flicked back to her and out to sea again. A man with something on his mind, she dubbed him. 'Zeb,' he said briefly, and since he hadn't mentioned his surname, she wondered since their meeting was to be fleeting if he thought it a waste of time supplying her with his surname.

But when he seemed to have looked long enough out to sea, he turned his attention back to her to ask, 'Is this your first time in Malta, Aldona?' and she knew he had no intention of using her surname either.

'Yes,' she said, and left it at that, not wanting him to ask her any more questions.

She was glad when he didn't, but showed himself very familiar with the island by telling her of places which she might find interesting on her visit, giving her a brief potted history of the Knights of St John as though he sensed straightaway she had a deep love of history. He told her about the Blue Grotto, the Tarxien temples, and was so interesting to listen to she could have stayed there for hours had he not looked across the beach and observed, as people began to drift indoors, that it must be getting near to feeding time.

Aldona knew then that this brief enchanting interlude was over. This half an hour or so spent in his company, when just by listening to him had taken her briefly out of her present-day reality, was at an end. Zeb stood up, but she stayed where she was. She didn't want to be seen entering the hotel with him. She hadn't left a note to say where she was going, hadn't known herself, but she didn't want Lionel Downs to come looking for her and to chance bumping into him and having to introduce the two men. She wanted this half hour to be hers, to be private, with nothing of her reason for being here to spoil it.

When she made no move to rise, he looked down at her, remarking, 'I shouldn't make a habit of sitting out too long without a hat.'

'I'll be going in presently,' she said.

Still he didn't go and she looked up to see him looking at her, a considering look on his face. She wondered what was going through his mind, and waited, that pounding in her heart starting up again. Then he frowned and said:

'If I can get hold of the party I want, my business shouldn't take long.' And then the frown disappeared and she saw he had strong white teeth as he charmed her with a smile and said, 'I should be free for dinner around nine. Have you got anything planned?'

Immediately she looked away. That smile was hard to resist. 'I'm—I'm not here by myself,' she said, and couldn't look at him to see what he made of that. There was a pause which lengthened, and she just couldn't raise her eyes.

'Lucky man,' he said at last, and the next time she looked up it was to see him striding away down the beach.

She sat for another ten minutes before moving—ample time, she thought, for him to have gone to his room. Then she got up.

Half expecting a display of more of Lionel's temper, for all she didn't see how he could object to her going out since he hadn't invited her to join him in a drink, Aldona opened the door of their room to see no sign of him. She listened outside the bathroom door in case he was in there having his bath before getting ready for dinner, and on hearing no sound opened the door pushing it inwards.

Relief sped through her to find he wasn't there. He'd had time to have more than one drink, but she didn't care how much he drank if it meant that while he was doing so she was spared his company.

Deciding that since she couldn't go down to dinner as she was, and that nothing was going to have her changing in the same room as Lionel, she took the long dress of tobacco brown from the wardrobe, together with fresh underclothes, into the bathroom, hanging her dress on the hook behind the door. Then she returned to the other room, taking the chair by the window, and sat looking out but not seeing anything.

It was ten past eight when the sound of someone at the door had her out of her chair and watching the door as Lionel came in. His face was florid, indicating that he had had several drinks in the time he had been away. But he was holding his alcohol well, and his speech was not slurred when he advanced into the room with a regretful look on his face that could have been pathetic had just looking at him not filled her with nausea.

'I've kept you waiting all this time,' he said, his stained yellow teeth much in evidence. 'Forgive me, sweetie. I met an old friend in the bar and he thought it would be a good idea if we went to this club he knew.'

'That's all right,' said Aldona, trying to look casual as she evaded him coming towards her and stepped to the other side of the chair out of his reach. Then, although not hungry, for all she had eaten very little that day, 'I did wonder about dinner, though.' She had fast come round from the view of not wanting to be seen with him, to thinking it was far preferable to be in the restaurant among other people, and that the longer she could keep him out of this room the better.

'You weren't thinking of going down dressed like that, were you, girlie?' he asked, his eyes going over her with that look she loathed.

'I was just waiting for you to come in before I changed,' she said, edging round the chair as he followed her. She reached the bathroom door without his touching her and was through, and closing the door to hear him say:

'If you have any zip trouble, let me know. I'm a dab hand with zips.'

Aldona eased the bolt home, trying to do it noiselessly, not wanting to give him any chance to take offence, then she leaned back against the door, sweat breaking out on her forehead, panic churning up her insides. Knowing her panic had to be mastered, she turned the shower full on, adjusting it so her hair wouldn't get wet, before she stepped out of her clothes and tried not to think at all as she let the water wash over her.

It had been impossible not to think, but if her mind was still weary her body was refreshed as she turned off the shower. Then instantly, her thoughts on the degradation that was to be hers were ousted as her ears picked up a commotion coming from the other room. There were voices talking in there—no, not talking, yelling, having one hell of a row, and she'd turned off the shower at the tail end by the sound of it as one roaring voice was shouting, 'I'll get you out if I die in the attempt!' Then Lionel Downs' voice, challenging, 'Do your worst, you can't hurt me without hurting her.' And the other voice, full of contempt, 'If you were a younger man ... ' Then a pause followed by the violent slamming of the door, the shock waves of which rattled the bathroom door. Then silence. The visitor, whoever he was, had gone.

Why she should think then of the man she had met on the beach, Aldona couldn't have said, for his well modulated tones had sounded nothing like the furiously hard, aggressive tones of the voice she had just heard. She pushed the image of him away. She didn't want to think about him either, only hoped against hope he wouldn't be in the dining room when she went in with Lionel Downs. She didn't want him to see her with her elderly escort, knowing he was shrewd enough to draw his own conclusions.

She dried and dressed, the words she had heard repeating themselves in her brain. Apparently Lionel Downs knew more than one person in Malta tonight, though anyone could have gathered from that heated exchange that his latest acquaintance could in no way be called a drinking friend. He must be a younger man too, if the intimation gathered from the threatened, 'If you were a younger man ...' was anything to go by, for clearly his visitor would have physically set about him had Lionel Downs been nearer his own age. And who was the woman Lionel Downs had said would be hurt if his aggressor did anything to get him out? And out of where? She gave it up. It was none of her business anyway and she certainly wasn't going to ask Lionel about it. She had no desire to know anything about him or the enemies he had made. She wanted no part of personal contact with him, no gradual learning more about him. The only way she was going to get through the next two weeks was by keeping her mind aloof from his. As for her body!

Her zip firmly in place, she left the bathroom and saw he had changed; presumably he had washed in one of the bathrooms she had noticed along the corridor. Fastidious about personal cleanliness herself, she sincerely hoped so, though she hardly thought it was of prior importance whether he had bathed or not.

'You're looking more beautiful than ever, girlie,' he said, coming towards her and grabbing hold of her bare arms with moist palms. 'Let's have a little kiss before we go down.'

Aldona saw his square face coming towards her, felt sick as she looked at his loose mouth, and gave a laugh that was near hysterical as her tummy chose that exact moment to rumble noisily, as she said urgently:

'Honestly, Mr—Lionel, I think I shall faint if I don't eat soon!'

Tension came back again as she waited for him to release her. For several awful seconds she thought he wasn't going to, thought she was going to have to put up with the feel of his wet mouth against her own. She had the insane idea that she would ruin everything if that happened, and that her natural instincts would win the day and she would be clawing and scratching at him. And then his hands dropped away and he was saying:

'Let's eat, then. The last thing I want is to have you fainting on me.'

Going to the restaurant, Aldona felt calmer and forced herself to think only of her father. Instructing her mind that when the time came, she must think only of him, think only of what it would mean to him if she didn't go through with this.

They were directed to a table for two, and she spent a considerable time looking through the menu. Food, she thought, would choke her, yet she had made such a thing of being hungry, she knew she would just have to eat. She chose fruit juice for her first course, and steak with salad for her second. If her stomach behaved she might finish with an ice cream, but for the moment she would see how she fared with each course as it came.

Lionel ordered wine to go with their meal, and was on his third glass while she was still sipping at her first, as she made an effort to get some of her steak down. In public at any rate he was behaving himself. Aldona had dreaded that he might think he had to touch her all the time as he had on the plane. She kept her eyes fixed either on her plate, or when she couldn't avoid it when he made some remark, flicking a glance at him, and forcing a smile as she recalled being taken to task for being 'hoity-toity'. Of the other diners she took no attention. She didn't want them to know her; she didn't want to know them.

Then she became aware that someone had come by their table and stopped. She thought it was the wine waiter with the second bottle of wine Lionel Downs had ordered, but when no wine was forthcoming she flicked her eyes upwards and the breath left her body. For there, standing as though frozen into immobility, stood the man she had met on the beach.

Only he wasn't the man she had met on the beach. That man had smiled and enchanted her with his talk of Malta. This man hadn't a smile in him, and as his glance went from her to her dinner partner and back to her again, it seemed to her that even his bronze tan had disappeared. There was a whiteness about his mouth anyway, as he gave her a look of searing contempt. Then she felt Lionel Downs' hot podgy hand over hers and she glanced away from the man who was Zeb, yet wasn't, and heard Lionel Downs say, 'Eat up, sweetie. I want to show you some night life before we go to bed.'

She just couldn't look at Zeb as the words told him clearly just what her relationship with her companion was. She looked down at Zeb's hands, saw his knuckles were white, his hands fists, then as though he had suddenly decided he was no longer hungry, he swung about and left the dining room.

Lionel Downs made no reference to the man who had paused by their table, but surely he must have noticed him? she thought. Or was it that because for some unknown reason Zeb had the power to make her heart beat faster, she had imagined his presence into giant proportions? She hadn't imagined that contemptuous look, though, she thought, as her heart settled down to a normal beat. He'd looked as though women of her sort turned his stomach, it had put him off his food anyway, though since the hotel had another restaurant he had probably chosen to eat there.

In the end the talk of showing her some of the night life didn't materialise. For they were making their way from the dining room when they bumped into another couple, a man about Lionel Downs' age, and a brassy blonde about ten years older than Aldona.

'Eddie,' Lionel Downs said instantly, 'you've sobered up from our session earlier, then?'

'Lionel, you old scoundrel!' the man Eddie proclaimed, his eyes taking in the beautiful dark-haired girl his friend was hanging on to. 'Aren't you going to introduce us to your—friend? This is Rosie, by the way.' Then, 'Look, we're cluttering up the doorway, let's go to the bar and have a drink.'

Two hours later they were still sitting in the four seats they had found inside the hotel bar. Aldona, who had seriously considered getting 'bombed out of her mind', to use one of the expressions she had heard Rosie Blake use, wondered if she drank herself senseless would it make her forthcoming ordeal any better for her, but she had found her father's teaching bringing her up short and had restricted herself to sipping a Martini. The other three were well on the way to getting plastered. She already had three Martinis lined up in front of her and despite her protests that she didn't want another one, Lionel Downs was again ordering a round that included yet another.

Eddie she didn't like at all; he was if anything cruder than Lionel. But Rosie wasn't so bad, and she managed to exchange one or two pleasantries with her when the two men were telling jokes that Rosie had either heard before or just wasn't interested in.

'Come on, Ally, drink up,' said Lionel, his eyes glassy, but a look of belligerence there that she wasn't joining in the party spirit.

'Your girl obviously wasn't brought up in the same fish tank as us,' Eddie cracked, and Lionel's belligerence changed to laughter as he took it as a compliment his friend that thought he could drink like a fish.

Eddie bought the next round, and a yawn escaped Aldona as boredom got the better of her. She wasn't a prude and had often sat, a Martini before her, in a pub with some of her friends. But she'd had something in common with them, had felt able to join in with their conversation. But here any remark she tried that wasn't directed solely at Rosie was taken up and a lewd connotation put on it, so that for the last half hour she had said nothing at all.

'Are you tired?' That was Lionel, sounding belligerent again, and the words rushed to Aldona's lips to deny tiredness as realisation came that to agree might have him saying it was time they called it a night.

'Travelling can be wearying,' Rosie put in, before she could answer, having learned that they had arrived that day. And as though she had discerned that Aldona was out of her element, 'Why don't you go up to bed, I'll stay down here and keep these two reprobates company.'

Aldona darted a quick look at Lionel to see how he was taking this suggestion, and saw from the way he beamed at Rosie that he enjoyed being called a reprobate, and again his belligerency fell away from him as he considered the suggestion with all the seriousness he could muster.

'Yes,' he said at length, 'you go up, sweetie, I'll stay on here for a bit.'

Relief flooding through her, Aldona got to her feet, saying a warm goodnight to Rosie, and doing the best she could in saying goodnight to the two men. Neither of the men stood up; she rather thought they would have fallen over if they tried it.

'We won't keep him down here too long,' Eddie's words followed her. She didn't look round to acknowledge that she had heard. As far as she was concerned if they kept him down there till breakfast time, it would be all right by her. Preferably for the whole two weeks.

CHAPTER THREE

ALDONA made no attempt to undress once she had reached the room, but sat down for some minutes staring bleakly in front of her. Agitatedly she stood up again and began to pace the room, then needing something to do she went into the bathroom and washed her face, then rinsed through the underwear she had worn that day, wringing the items almost dry in a hand towel, then rather than leave her washing hanging about, found a fresh towel and rolled her laundry inside and popped it inside her case. The trepidation she was feeling had her thinking that if there was the smallest chance of her not being awakened by a hot podgy paw when Lionel Downs came to bed, then she would be between the covers quicker than that and feigning sleep, even if she was to lie wide awake. But she had witnessed enough of him to know that such a nicety as leaving her to sleep undisturbed would never occur to him, so she went and tidied the bathroom, then resumed her pacing up and down.

Her heart began hammering with fear when she heard a noise in the corridor outside, and at a knocking on the door, she went to open it. She opened it wide when she saw Lionel Downs propped up between a porter on one side and Rosie on the other, though Rosie didn't look any too steady on her feet as she grinned at Aldona foolishly and said:

'We've just dropped Eddie off—where do you want this cargo?'

Aldona politely thanked the porter for his assistance as he took the bulk of the weight and dropped Lionel on the nearest of the two beds before, his face inscrutable as though he'd done this sort of job many times, he departed.

Rosie seemed familiar with the routine too, for even in her tipsy state she had taken off Lionel's shoes and loosened his tie, before staggering back into an upright position and holding on to the dressing table while she got Aldona into focus.

'He'll not bother you tonight, duckie,' she said, going to grope for the door, which had Aldona going to open it for her. 'He'll sleep till well past midday, if I'm any judge.'

Aldona found Rosie's words cheering, though she was not sure how much faith she could put on them. Then she looked at Lionel, dead to the world with only a loud snore being emitted from time to time to say he would be resurrected when the effects of the alcohol he had consumed wore off. He looked no more prepossessing asleep than he did awake. She put out the light, took off her shoes and, still in her dress, lay down on the other bed.

She had felt tired enough to sleep the clock round, but some subconscious alarm told her even in sleep that things were not right and had her waking at dawn. The sound of snoring had her looking at the other bed. Lionel was still sound asleep, but she knew she wouldn't be going back to sleep.

Taking care not to make a noise, she eased herself off the bed, carefully extracted underclothes from a drawer and the slacks and shirt she had worn yesterday, and not wanting to risk the sound of running water waking him, she left the room and headed for one of the bathrooms up the corridor. When she had bathed and changed she then wrapped her dinner dress and other garments in a towel so that should anyone be about at this hour they would think she was going for an early morning swim.

One or two of the hotel staff were about, and wished her a pleasant, 'Good morning,' to which she replied pleasantly in return, then she was outside and having the small private beach to herself.

She made for the spot where she had sat yesterday, musing that she wouldn't be seeing Zeb again. He had booked in for only one night and would probably be away once he had had his breakfast. And in view of his contemptuous look last night she had no intention of going in to breakfast herself and risking bumping into him. She was on the point of wondering if Lionel Downs slept until lunch time, as Rosie seemed to think he would. Could she put off going back into that room she was beginning to hate until perhaps after he had pulled himself off the bed, and with luck, gone for another drinking session with Eddie? A movement to the side of her had her turning to see the man she had thought she would never see again walking along the beach. She knew he had seen her, but after that look he had given her last night, she knew also that he was going to ignore her as though she wasn't there.

In that she was wrong. He was almost past her when he stopped. He was some ten yards away when he turned and just stood there looking at her. It came to her mind to stand up and walk back to the hotel, to ignore him, for she was suddenly sure from the hard look of him that if he had anything he wanted to say to her then it would be something far from pleasant. And she had just about had her fill of things unpleasant.

But what would she do once inside the hotel? It was too early for breakfast, and she had just realised that after only picking at her meals yesterday with the pressure of Lionel Downs' company temporarily lifted, she was hungry. She stayed where she was and refused to lower her eyes when, not taking his eyes from her, Zeb moved from the spot where he had been standing staring aggressively at her. He walked towards her, his casual gait at variance with the harshness on his face. He stopped when his feet were almost touching hers and there was no sign of the smile he had given her yesterday as he looked her over, then spoke, his voice pure acid, his tones scathing.

'Just how much is your *husband* paying you for your services?' he asked, his question direct and making no apology for it.

'H-husband?' she queried huskily, already feeling the disadvantage of being seated while he was towering over her.

'There's no Aldona Mayhew in the hotel's register,' he said, causing her to stare at him that he had bothered to look, until what he said next had her thinking it wasn't her name he had been looking for. 'But there is a Lionel Downs booked in, with *wife*.'

In what name Lionel Downs had booked her in had been the lesser of her worries yesterday. She just hadn't thought about it. And knowing now that she was supposed to be Mrs Downs didn't have the full impact it might have done as the suspicion came that the man who was speaking so slightingly to her had checked the hotel register looking for Lionel Downs' name. Had Lionel Downs been the person he had spoken of as having business with? She recalled the tail end of the row she had overheard and was suddenly convinced that the other voice, heard and not recognised because it had been raised in anger, belonged to this man who was glowering down at her. But before her lips could frame the question, he was asking:

'And where is your husband now?'

'In bed,' she answered, though on top of it would have been more accurate, and before he could put another of his direct questions, 'You know him, don't you? You were

in ...' Her question of was he in the room yesterday with
Lionel was cut short, her previous question of did he know
him ignored altogether, as he repeated his question of
how much was she being paid for her services.

'Downs must be going to pay you,' he said stingingly
when she didn't answer. 'He hasn't got that much to
recommend him that a girl with your looks would shack
up with him unless there was something very worthwhile
at the end of it for her.'

It passed her by that he thought her looks were worth
a mention. Didn't she have enough on her plate without
having her few snatched moments of solitude intruded
upon so aggressively? Who did he think he was anyway
that he could just come up to her on a deserted beach
and lay into her as if she was of no account? And what
the devil was it to do with him? Having felt for too long
as though the sins of the world were heaped on her
shoulders, she was suddenly fed up with having to go
around with shame in her heart, with avoiding other
people's glances, of looking the other way when anyone
showed the least sign of a holiday smile in her direction,
and pride roared in. It had her lifting her head and saying:

'What's it to you? Nobody's asking you to pay the bill.'
She saw his eyes narrow that she had come back fighting,
and tacked on carelessly, 'And for your information, I
don't have to wait until the—holiday is over. I've been
paid in advance.'

'Naturally,' was the sharp response. 'Forgive me for
overlooking that point. You're a girl with her head screwed
on the right way, aren't you? You've probably learned
from previous experience that once the ardour has cooled
there might be some quibbling over the amount.' Aldona's
pride wavered as nausea she was fast growing accustomed
to feeling gripped at her stomach. 'How much was the

amount—you never said?' Zeb asked again.

He seemed intent on learning how much she was selling her favours for, and she was grateful that her pride hadn't deserted her altogether. It made her able to look back at him and say, quite brazenly, she thought:

'Why the interest? You're hardly likely to want to be a contender, even if you could afford it.' The way he was now looking at her told her that, and if it didn't she had the added reminder of the contemptuous way he had looked at her last night. Oh, why didn't he go and leave her in peace? She had gone right off the idea of having breakfast.

'I don't know about that,' he said after long moments of silence when Aldona could no longer meet his steady gaze and was looking anywhere but at him. 'I reckon I can bid higher than Downs.'

She knew he was waiting for her to tell him how much Lionel Downs had paid for her, and felt incredulous that she, Aldona Mayhew, who lived what a lot of people might call a plain humdrum life—though she had always thought herself happy in the things she had done, the most eventful so far being engaged for six weeks—should find herself in the position she was in, and not only that, but that she should find herself bandying words, quite brazenly, she thought, on a subject that was not only disgusting and offensive to her moral code, but finding that she hadn't taken to her heels and fled the moment he had asked his first question.

'His cheque was for two thousand pounds,' she heard herself say, to her further incredulity. But her incredulity was far outmatched by his as the exclamation broke from him:

'Two thousand? Ye gods! You must have something pretty special.'

Aldona looked round for her towelled bundle; she had had enough. She'd vomit if she stayed here another second. 'You'll never know, will you?' she said with a coolness that amazed her, and her hand reaching for the white towelling was arrested as he said consideringly:

'I don't know about that.' Her eyes flew to him to discover his eyes going over her, leaving her face and travelling over her slender form, his glance resting on the curve of her breasts outlined beneath her thin cotton shirt. 'I'm not a poor man,' he told her, his eyes leaving her bust line to go to her mouth and then to her wide brown eyes. 'I reckon I can outmatch the asking price.' She just sat and stared at him, astonishment uppermost that this man was calmly talking to her as if she was an exhibit at some fat stock market. 'Though first I'd want to sample the goods.'

Sample the goods! His insulting words penetrated and she was unsure which she wanted to do first, pummel him with her fists until she had attempted to knock him senseless, or throw up on the spot. In a second she was on her feet. This conversation had gone much too far.

But she had made a big mistake in bringing her height to a nearer level with his, though he still topped her by a good eight inches. For as she would have turned and fled, he caught hold of her.

'Customer's prerogative, I believe,' he said, and ignored her when she began to struggle at what she thought his intention was. He pulled her closer and she felt the hardness of his body up against her own. And while her wide brown eyes said 'No', and her struggle to break his iron grip became more agitated, his head came down and firm warm lips were over hers.

She pushed and tried to kick out at him when he refused to let her go, but her efforts were puny compared with his strength. She kicked out at him again, but found her feet kicking air as her aim failed to connect, and all she achieved was to lose her balance so that it was easy for him to hold her pushing backwards until they were both lying on the sand, Zeb's mouth still over hers.

He broke his kiss to catch at her flailing hands, tucking one of her arms under his body as he rolled to lie half on top of her, his right leg battening down her legs, his right hand pinning her one free hand to the sand.

'Lie back and enjoy it,' he said softly. 'Show me what you're made of, *Mrs Downs*.'

Even while savouring what she'd got to offer he was still insulting, and Aldona tried to arch her body to force him away from her. But that too was a mistake, for her body came into even closer contact with his and his superior strength retaliated by keeping that contact close when she would have shrunk away from him.

'Let me up!' she exclaimed furiously, and those were the last words she spoke for some time, as the light was blocked out and Zeb's mouth again found hers.

Only this time, instead of making his kiss insulting, he set about getting her to respond. His lips, still firm, were not hard against hers, but mobile, sensuous, and his body fluid where before the pressure had been hurting her.

His mouth left hers and when she would have berated him and demanded that he let her go, she felt his lips teasing at the back of her ear, felt a disturbing sensation begin to grow in her as he kissed her throat, that had nothing to do with the anger she had experienced when he had first hauled her to him, and no word left her, so that by the time he again claimed her lips, the moment had gone when she could have given rein to what she thought of him.

How he got her to part her lips, she didn't know. She wasn't conscious of him having to force them apart. All she was conscious of was a tingling thrill of pleasure that was growing within her that had to be firmly stepped on if she didn't want him to be convinced she didn't care who she sold her favours to if the price was right.

And then, just when the battle against the treacherous feelings Zeb was arousing in her body was at its height, she found herself free as his mouth left hers and he moved to his side where he lay looking down at her.

'As a sample, that wasn't bad,' he drawled, looking in no way as if he had experienced those same disturbing sensations she had felt. 'Though I'm sure if you tried harder, you could do better. However ...'

'However nothing!' snapped Aldona, rapidly coming to life and realising that she had at some point back there ceased in her struggles and he was now definitely of the opinion he wouldn't have to work on her long to get her full co-operation. She put out her hands to assist her to sit up, found the towelling bundle underneath one of them and gathered it to her as she got to her feet. 'You've wasted your time sampling the product, Mr...' She didn't know his other name, and she was feeling far too unfriendly to use the one she did know.

'Have I?' he queried sardonically.

'Yes, you have,' she said flatly, not wanting to hear another word from him. 'You're leaving today. I'm here for another two weeks. So I'm afraid it's a case of never the twain shall meet, and I for one will run up the flag that I shall never have to see you again.'

If he had anything to say in answer to that, she wasn't waiting around to hear it. Walking quickly, restraining the impulse to run, she left him sitting there. Whether he was looking after her she neither knew nor cared. What she did know was that never had she ever been kissed so thoroughly, so expertly, and—admit it, so marvellously in her whole life.

She saw the breakfast room was open when she entered the hotel and went in purely because she needed a cup of coffee and had a decided aversion to going to that room upstairs. She sat where she could see the door, intending to get up and leave if Zeb came in. But, her first cup of coffee finished, she began to unwind. And deciding that even if he did come in, he wouldn't come and sit down at her table, she poured herself another cup of coffee and ordered a slice of toast to go with it.

She stayed in the breakfast room as long as she dared without making herself look conspicuous, her mind going over the things Zeb had said to her on the beach. Of course he wasn't really interested in taking her over from Lionel Downs; it was just his way of trying to make her feel cheap. If only he knew! That had been achieved without any help from him.

Thinking, as people came into breakfast and then left, that she had spent long enough sitting at her table, she wondered what to do next. She had been stupid enough to leave her handbag upstairs and had no inclination to go and collect it in case Lionel was awake. She opted to go into the lounge and spent a good deal of the morning buried behind newspapers left behind by other patrons of the hotel.

She did think of leaving the hotel and exploring the island, but there were two things against that. One, she hadn't any money with her, and two, should Lionel have awakened and have turned nasty that she wasn't there, she could honestly say she had stayed in the hotel, and less honestly, that she had thought he would sleep more soundly if she wasn't there to disturb him.

Towards lunch time, she expected every figure who came to the lounge doorway to be him, and when an hour later he hadn't shown himself, her appetite made itself felt and she went in to lunch.

Around three o'clock she became aware that her head had begun to ache, and didn't have to look very far for the cause. She just knew she couldn't put off going up to that room any longer. But oh, how she wished she could!

Lionel was sitting on the bed as she went in, looking every bit the morning after, as he deserved, for it was now afternoon, looking through his shifty bloodshot eyes as though he had only just awakened, and not wakened in a very sunny mood either.

'Where the hell have you been?' he demanded when she had closed the door and dropped her towelling bundle down on the dressing table. 'The chambermaid woke me up earlier and you weren't here.'

'I didn't want to disturb you by moving around,' Aldona trotted out, 'so I went to sit in the lounge.'

Lionel didn't thank her for her consideration—she hadn't expected him to—but passed a dry tongue over his lips, then looked at her, his eyes greedy. 'Come here,' he ordered, and Aldona's heart began to pound in fear, setting up a counterpoint to her throbbing head.

'I—I have a headache,' she stammered, bringing out the first excuse she could think of, though a very real one.

'So have I,' was the unrelenting reply. 'Come here.'

She froze, petrified where she stood. Had her life depended on it she couldn't have moved then as the overweight man ponderously got up from the bed and lumbered towards her.

'You'll come to my bed if I have to drag you to it,' he said lasciviously, catching hold of her and pulling her with him, and being twice her weight manhandled her until he had hauled her to the bed.

Terror mixed with hysteria had hold of her, and she knew at that point if it meant the death of her father, then she just couldn't go through with it.

'No!' she screamed as his hands went to the fastenings of her clothes. 'No, I can't!'

'Yes, you can—and you damn well will,' was the reply. 'I've waited long enough for you, girlie, I'm not waiting any longer.'

Beside herself with terror, Aldona looked round for a weapon to hit him with, but there was nothing near. And as her hands fought to keep Lionel's podgy paws away from her he seemed to lose his balance, and for a very few seconds her body and limbs were free of his bulk.

Those few seconds were all she needed, and like lightning she was off the bed and at the door, her fingers curling round the door handle. She had kept her eyes on him in her flight, and paused, a shaky breath escaping her as she stood by the door, safe for the moment that he hadn't moved, and gaining a semblance of calm from the knowledge that she was much lighter on her feet and would be moving twice as fast as him if he took one step towards her.

'I—I can't do it,' she said croakily when he stayed where he was. 'I'm—I'm sorry Mr—Lionel, I thought I could—but I can't.'

'You've left it a bit late in the day to find that out, girlie,' he said, breathing heavily, from his exertions, she hoped. 'I say you can and you will. Don't forget I still have the power to put your old man in prison,' he went ruthlessly on, 'so either you come across or I'll finish him.'

'But—but he's got your cheque for two thousand pounds,' she protested, distractedly noting that shifty-eyed look was with him at her words, and wondering how she could ever have thought a few moments earlier that she could allow her father to die.

'And I want value for that two thousand,' he said, then leered because he knew he had the trump card. 'Either you keep to the bargain we made or you return my money with interest,' he muttered, his breathing not easing as he looked at her slight trembling form by the door.

'*Please!*' she pleaded, ready to beg if need be. 'Please don't make me go through with this!'

She knew she was wasting her time in trying to appeal to his better nature and her fingers clenched round the door handle, ready to wrench the door open if he but so much as stood up.

'Since you don't want to honour the agreement we made in London, I'll make a fresh bargain with you,' he offered, and she could see from the cunning light in his eyes that he was enjoying himself hugely at her expense.

'What—what sort of bargain?' she asked, knowing from the look of him that she was foolish to let hope rise within her.

'You pay me three thousand before bedtime tonight and I'll forget that I ever fancied you.'

'Three thousand?' she repeated, not knowing why she did, because he might as well have asked for ten thousand for all the hope she had of getting it.

'I said I wanted my money back with interest, didn't I?' Lionel reminded her, and stood up. It was a signal for her to turn the door handle. 'Now come on, sweetie,' he said, his voice oily, the greedy light for her there in his eyes again. 'We both know you haven't a hope of getting that money. Come over here and pay your dues.' He took a step towards her. It was all that was needed to have Aldona pulling the door open and speeding through it.

How she came to be wandering about on the next floor up, she had no idea. She had no recollection of using the stairs or the lift, only a recollection of Lionel's fat fingers on her and that had been enough to give her feet wings. Maybe some instinct of self-preservation had made her feet speed upwards instead of down, she thought, her flight at an end as she leaned against the wall and tried to get her chaotic thoughts into order. It would be natural for Lionel to think she would go downstairs if he came after her.

She drew a shuddering breath and thought, oh, he was awful! She just couldn't go through with it—yet she must. A dry sob left her, then before she could draw another breath the door to the left of her opened and she had another shock when she found herself face to face with the man who had insulted her on the beach that morning. Lost for words she just stared at him.

'Well, well,' he drawled sardonically. 'Have you come looking for me?' Then, his eyes narrowing as he looked into her white face, he added, 'By the look of you, you need a drink. Come in.'

Vaguely Aldona was aware of being propelled unprotestingly into his room, some part of her mind reasoning she hadn't expected to see him again, she had thought he would have checked out by now. And then Zeb was pushing her into a chair and handing her a glass of what smelt like Scotch.

She took a sip of the drink merely because she needed time to pull herself together. The whisky fired at her throat, but she managed to swallow down the choking cough that took her as she saw Zeb was half standing, half leaning against a chest, his hands in his pockets, the material of his trousers against his thighs straining against the muscles there. No spare flesh on him, she thought, not like ... She took another sip of her drink, wanting to drown the memory of those fat fingers.

Unspeaking, Zeb surveyed her. She guessed he was waiting for her to recover so she could tell him what she was doing up on his floor since he must know her room number, having checked the hotel register. And not only that, if her suspicions were right about his involvement in that row, then he had been in that room.

'I—er—didn't come up here looking for you,' she told him, when the silent way he was surveying her had her nerve ends jangling. 'I thought you'd checked out.'

She expected him to say something to that, but he volunteered no information as to what he was doing by still being there. Not a muscle moved as he waited for her to continue. The thought crossed her mind to tell him she had taken it into her head to explore the hotel. But the strong intelligence in his face told her he wasn't going to believe that, would be scathing about her lies when he had seen for himself she had been leaning as though shaken and exhausted against the corridor wall.

'I—er—had a bit of—a spat with—Lionel,' she said at last, wishing her limbs felt stronger so she could just hand him back his glass and disappear. Then found she did have enough strength to get to her feet when he asked sarcastically:

'Do I hear the strains of discord in your love nest?' He straightened up too then, but only so he could lean forward and push her back into her chair, remarking, 'You're still pale, sit there for a while.'

Aldona doubted he had any regard whatsoever for whether she was pale or not. Rather she thought he was more intent on finding out what her quarrel had been about—though she couldn't think why he should be interested unless he had been the man with the angry voice shouting at Lionel Downs, then it would most likely give him a lot of pleasure to know that things weren't going all that smoothly for him. But she was glad to be sitting down again. Her head was pounding, and she was suffering a reaction from that scene down on the next floor.

A morose sort of silence seemed to fill the room, then into the silence came the question, 'What was your "spat" about?' a question she didn't want to answer. She didn't want to tell him and have to relive that vile scene. She wanted to forget all that had happened, wanted the moments spent in freedom from that room not to have reminders that something of a similar nature was going to happen the moment she returned, as she knew she must.

An involuntary shudder took her as she recalled the lustful way Lionel had dragged her on to the bed. And she had to return to that! Unless she could find three thousand pounds before tonight she would have to ... Her thoughts broke off. Heaven help her, she prayed, where was she going to get three thousand pounds?

And then, just as though her prayers were answered, she looked at the man standing in front of her, and the words he had spoken only that morning came hurtling into her head. 'I reckon I can bid higher than Downs.'

Her eyes widened with amazement at the direction her thoughts were taking. From the frying pan into the fire wasn't in it! She hadn't answered his question as to what her spat with Lionel had been about. But as she looked at him, tall, cynical, arrogant, but oh, so much nearer her own age—about thirty-five, she thought—she remembered the way his kiss had disturbed her and knew, sick though the idea was, that if she had to sell her body to someone, and remembering her father with his suspect heart, what choice did she have, then impossible though she was going to find it to live with herself afterwards, she was going to have much less difficulty if that man was some-one who had something to recommend him.

'Er——' she began, and found that while her question was urgent, she just couldn't voice it.

'I've been watching your face,' she was told, when it

was obvious she had nothing to add. 'From appearing to be a shaken young woman with an air of desperation about you, you look as though you've suddenly had a bright idea that'll be to your advantage if it comes off.' His expression wasn't very inviting as he ordered, 'Out with it Aldona, I'm not easily shocked.'

He had said he wasn't a poor man either, but had that been true? His clothes looked expensive, his shoes hand-made, and though he was inviting her thoughts, Aldona wasn't sure he didn't think her air of desperation he had witnessed was all one big act.

'Er——' she said again, then knowing whatever he thought of her, she just had to ask him, she lowered her eyes, forcing herself to speak slowly and coolly. 'On the beach you said you could bid higher than—than Downs.' Oh, this was awful, she knew she was making a fool of herself, but the desperation he had spoken of seeing was real. The very air about her felt cold as she forced the rest of her words into the freezing silence. 'D-did you mean it?' The air crackled with arctic frostbite as she closed her eyes and waited for Zeb to pitch her out on her ear.

CHAPTER FOUR

HER mind seemed to be suspended, no thoughts at all coming through as she waited for Zeb to voice his disgust with her. She didn't have to wait very long, and though she could hear a thread of distaste in his voice, he didn't, as she had anticipated, pick her up and throw her bodily out into the hall.

'It would appear that the formula Downs is using isn't

the right one to stir your blood,' he said nastily, not answering her question at all. 'What's the matter, Aldona? Have you suddenly discovered two thousand pounds isn't enough for putting up with him mauling you around, listening to his asthmatic breathing while he's making love to you, seeing his figure flabby when undressed?'

Aldona made to stand up, but was pushed unceremoniously down again as Zeb left the chest he was leaning against and came to stand over her. In a way she supposed she deserved all he was saying, and she was rather shocked at what she had asked him, but then anything was preferable to ...

Helpless, knowing she was going nowhere until he had decided to let her out of her chair, she looked up at him. She saw the look of disgust his expression held for her and lifted her chin a few degrees higher. Her pride had been sunk without trace, but something was struggling within her that said when she did leave this room it would be with as much dignity as possible.

'I apologise for my question,' she said quietly. 'Obviously I misjudged the situation. If you'll stand out of my way, I shan't bother you again.'

Zeb didn't stand out of her way, but eyed her levelly for a moment, and she flinched as though struck when he asked dryly, 'Thinking of plying your trade elsewhere?' and as her face went ashen, and her stomach gripped, she saw his look turn from her, an expression crossing his face as though he too considered his words a blow beneath the belt for all what she had done could be read that way.

He made no apology however, but turned his attention back to her, then said consideringly, 'I've never gone in for giving actual cash for—favours received.' Aldona could only gather from that that perhaps an item of jewellery or something similar had been his kind of thank-you, but had no time to allow her thoughts licence in that direction, for he was going on as he insultingly looked her over, 'Though from what I remember of kissing you this morning, I wouldn't be averse to giving you a tumble.'

Aldona was feeling more defeated by the minute. She was sure Zeb didn't usually speak to his women friends in this rough manner, but knew she couldn't expect any better when she had clearly given him the impression that she was a trollop of the first water.

'You wouldn't?' She forced the question, knowing if she was to get his agreement she would have to participate in this nauseating conversation, but her agitation mindblowing at the thought of having to stay with Lionel Downs. Whatever happened some instinct was telling her, this man's lovemaking wouldn't be a sweating, laboured, grabbing possession. Tears sprang to her eyes and had to be checked if Zeb was to continue to believe she was the hard case she was making out to be.

'If I take you over,' he said thoughtfully, 'you'll have to move in with me, sever all connections with Downs.'

Willingly, she thought, though couldn't understand the look of pleasure that crossed his face. It wasn't at the prospect of having her in his bed, she felt sure about that. And she was positive suddenly that it *had* been he who had been rowing with Lionel, and that look of pleasure was purely from the anticipated satisfaction he would get from taking her away from him, the girl Lionel Downs had looked forward to spending a cosy two weeks with. She wished her head would stop aching so she could remember what she had heard of that row, but with this present discussion needing so much of her attention, nothing was coming through.

'That will be all right,' she agreed as calmly as she could, and when Zeb had her agreement to that part of her new contract, he said:

'That leaves only one other point, I think. You referred to my bidding higher. Do I gather from that that the asking price has jumped somewhat?'

Why she should feel like hitting him for his cynicism Aldona didn't know, for he was only stating what he would soon know was fact. But she was glad to experience that bubble of aggression, having felt for too long the feeling of being backed into a corner with no way out.

'I thought three thousand?' she said, and could have blushed that she brought it out without a stammer. Perhaps I'm getting case-hardened, she thought, and wanted to giggle, and knew then that she was on the verge of hysteria if she didn't watch herself.

To his credit Zeb didn't bat an eyelid at the amount, though he did throw her a look that gave her the distinct impression that women like her made him sick. Endorsing for her that her as a woman he could take or leave, but not the chance to put one over on Lionel Downs.

'Er—can I have the money in advance?' she asked, making no move to go and pack her case and return to this room as she thought he would be expecting.

'It's your usual custom, isn't it?' he drawled, and went to the wardrobe, taking out a jacket and extracting a cheque book and pen.

'W-would you make it out to cash, please,' she said when he uncapped his fountain pen and looked ready to write. It would only complicate matters if the cheque was made out to her when she handed it over.

It took him no time at all to fill in the cheque, but when Aldona went to take it from him, she saw that it was two cheques he was giving her. She looked at him with a question in her eyes.

'There's one cheque there for two thousand made out to Downs. That I think buys you from him.' So he wouldn't be in debt to any man, she thought. 'The other is for a thousand made out for cash as you asked.'

He looked ready to go for her if she was about to argue that she didn't think much of him doing her out of two thousand pounds. But before she could say anything, and all that was in her mind to say was a polite thank-you, he changed his mind about giving her the two cheques and handed over only one.

'On second thoughts, I'll come with you,' he said, and for a moment Aldona thought it was because he didn't trust her to hand over the two thousand cheque. Then it dawned on her that the score he had to settle with Lionel Downs was eating away at him, and it would give him very great satisfaction to see his face when he took her away from him.

But she couldn't have that. The idea of going back to that room alone was going to take all her courage. But she was doing this for her father and since Zeb and Lionel must be acquainted with each other, she didn't want them to get into an argument about her where it might be revealed how she came to be in Malta. It was bad enough that Lionel Downs knew what her father had done. If Zeb knew too, he would be another person with some hold on her. When her time here was over she wanted the whole nightmare to be dead and buried.

'No,' she said flatly, 'I can't allow you to do that.' And then looking for a sensitivity in him she wasn't sure he had, she said, 'I owe it to him to tell him privately.' She was sure he was going to overrule her, and it was panic that her father's disgrace should be known by only one other man that had her daring, 'Either I do it my way—or not at all.'

Zeb looked at her long and hard, then when she just knew he was going to say, 'Not at all,' he suddenly capitulated. His look was shrewd, but he handed the other cheque over. Aldona didn't bother looking at either cheque. Strangely she trusted him to have written them the way he had said. She folded them in half, then stood up wondering what sort of exit line one used in the circumstances.

'I'll—er—see you later,' she said, and caught the tail end of his mocking look as she walked to the door.

She was glad Lionel Downs wasn't there when she got back, her headache began to ease off and with his shifty-eyed glances not following her, she was able to pack without keeping a wary eye open in case he made a grab for her. She hoped she wasn't in for an argument when he returned, but it was he who had stated he would let her go if she found the three thousand he had asked for. For three thousand pounds, he had said he would forget he fancied her. He had said too that he still had the power to put her father in prison. She'd have to get that settled before she left, but ...

The door opened just as she was clicking the latch on her suitcase into place, and all thoughts sped as she saw Lionel Downs come in, his eyes going to her case as he closed the door behind him.

'What's going on?' he asked, belligerence to the fore, telling her she wasn't in for an easy time.

'We made a fresh bargain,' she said, forcing herself to keep calm, to keep her voice steady. She pointed to the two cheques on the dressing table afraid to go near him until he said he was ready to abide by their new bargain. 'There's the three thousand you asked for—I'm leaving.'

'You're leaving!' the exclamation broke from him as his eyes went to the two cheques. She saw his podgy fingers take them up as though he couldn't credit what she was saying. Then another exclamation exploded from him as he looked at them. 'Good lord!' he said, and it was Aldona's turn to be startled as she wondered if she should have studied the cheques, the signature, she didn't even know Zeb's other name. But that wasn't important—he hadn't been making a fool of her had he?

'The cheques,' she said, her voice growing hoarse. 'They are for three thousand pounds, aren't they?'

There was another sort of look in Lionel's eyes, a look she could have read that his avarice was as much for money as it was to possess her, only that didn't make sense for at the start he had parted with his own two thousand pounds for her without any argument. And then the expression left his face so that she thought she must have imagined it.

'Oh yes,' he said, his eyes going over her, 'they add up to three thousand quid all right. So Zeb's cutting me out, is he?'

Here was an opportunity to ask him to tell her what he knew of Zeb, but apart from the sneering way he had said Zeb's name, indicating there was no love lost on either side, she didn't trust that look in his eyes that mentally stripped her, and there was only one other thing she had to get straightened out before she got out of here.

He advanced towards her, but she had made sure the chair separated them. 'My father,' she said. 'Do I have your word that he's now in the clear?'

'Your father?' said Lionel Downs absently, as though he had forgotten he had ever existed as he came nearer, the cheques too forgotten, and at that distance Aldona could see nothing in his eyes but lust.

Even while judging if he came round the chair after her, she could still make it to the door before him, she was forced to stay where she was until she had his word about her father.

'My father,' she repeated, forcing herself to hold his eyes. 'You said you still had the power to put him in prison. You won't, will you, not now you have your money back and an extra thousand?'

The lust in his eyes faded momentarily as he recalled the cheques in his possession. And his mind more on the money than anything, she thought, he told her, 'You need have no fears for your old man from me, girlie, his character will stay as white as the driven snow.'

It was all she wanted to hear, but as she bent to pick up her case, he lunged after her, grabbing at her hand in an attempt to pull her towards him, and Aldona knew she wasn't out of the wood yet, not until she was through that door.

'Just one kiss, my pet—now that's not too much to ask after all I've done for your father, is it?'

It wasn't. And if she thought she could have trusted him, knowing she would never have to see him again— she'd change the night she visited her father from Wednesdays—she might well have suffered herself to kiss him. But she didn't trust him. She knew full well that if she ever got entangled in those flabby arms, he wouldn't let her go until he had taken more than a kiss.

She didn't answer, but gave one gigantic pull to get her hand away from him, caught him unawares since it must have looked as though she was considering his latest proposition, and she was at the door, had it open before he bounded up behind her, pulling at the collar of her shirt and half yanking it over her shoulder.

And then as he pulled her away from the door and her heart began to pound with a fear she had known before, Lionel went to slam the door. Only he couldn't close it, for there was an object in the way, an object in the shape of a well-made shoe.

As she followed his disbelieving gaze, Aldona's expression became disbelieving too. Then all fear left her and she could have cried in relief. For Zeb stood there, his one glance taking in the scene. He then stepped over to where she was standing pale-faced and shaking, and just as though she were a nine-year-old he was dressing for school, he righted her shirt on her shoulder. With cool fingers he buttoned up the button at the swell of her breasts that had been forced from its moorings, then turning to Lionel Downs, his face as though carved from ice, he said, 'My merchandise, I believe,' then pushing her shoulder bag into her hands, he promptly picked up her case that had gone thudding to the floor when a grab at her had been made, and coolly shepherded her from the room.

Had she thought about it, Aldona would have known she would eventually have had to pay for all the trauma that had gone on within her ever since that visit to her father last Wednesday. Had she given the matter any thought, she would have been inclined to the view that she'd be lucky if she didn't end up with a nervous breakdown. But she hadn't thought about it and it wasn't until Zeb, who hadn't spoken a word since they had vacated that room on the other floor, ushered her into the room she was to share with him for the remainder of his stay—and she had no clue to how long that was likely to be—that her vision blurred, and stayed blurred for all she blinked to clear it. She knew then, from that swimming sensation that had happened only once before, that she was in for the mother and father of a migraine attack.

Her vision wavery, she found herself in a chair she thought was the one she had sat in before, but couldn't be sure. Then her vision went altogether, though she wasn't too alarmed by it, not nearly as alarmed as she had been the first time it had happened. She closed her eyes, resting her head against the back of the chair and recalling her fear that other time. It had been after trauma then too. After all her anxieties of first learning that her father had been rushed to hospital with a heart attack. After days and nights of him being in intensive care. It had been after a week of constant anxiety, of being afraid to leave the hospital in case his condition deteriorated, when she had at last been told he was being moved out of intensive care into one of the quiet but less specialised wards. Though it was early days, she had been told he was making progress and should make it. She had still been in the hospital grounds when her vision had gone, and some kindly soul had taken her to Casualty.

She recognised her symptoms now, wondered fleetingly if it was because she had been rescued from Lionel Downs that her inner consciousness had let up—as though it recognised she was out of that danger of knowing she couldn't have lived with herself afterwards. Why it was failing to recognise that she was still in a traumatic situation, that tonight she would be sharing that double bed she had noticed in the room on her other visit with her new temporary owner—his merchandise, he had called her—she didn't know. What she did know, and remembered from the doctor in Casualty telling her, was that she was starting a migraine and that once it had started there was nothing she could do about it but let it take its course.

The pain began. She heard Zeb moving about; it sounded like a herd of elephants. What he was doing she didn't know. She cared even less as the feeling of wanting to be sick hit her stomach.

'Have you any soluble aspirin?' she heard her voice ask on a whisper.

'It's a bit early in the evening to pull the headache routine, isn't it?' asked a cynical-sounding voice.

She heard him moving, but kept her eyes closed. Then when she didn't answer his taunt, she heard him move again, and felt he was much nearer. Had an impression he was standing over her looking down at her, but there

was no point in opening her eyes to find out, she knew
there was only blackness out there. She heard him suck
in his breath, every sound magnified as migraine took hold.

'Do you always go that pale green colour when you have
a headache?' he remarked, letting her know on seeing the
colour of her skin he was now prepared to believe she
wasn't faking.

'It's migraine,' she said, wanting to do nothing more
than lie down.

She didn't know if he knew anything about migraine or
not, but for all she guessed his voice hadn't been raised,
it was very quiet when he instructed her, not ungently,
she thought:

'Get into bed, I'll rustle up the aspirin.'

She heard him move away and tried to get to her feet.
But pain shot through her and she knew coping with that
and finding where the bed was if she wasn't in the chair
she thought she was, was going to be more of an effort
than she was up to. She had her eyes open when he came
back, but it wasn't her sense of vision that told her he
was there. He had moved noiselessly, but something told
her he was standing in front of her.

'Wouldn't you be better off in bed?' he asked. Then,
'Don't you want your aspirin after all?' She could only
gather from that that he was holding a glass or something
out to her.

'I can't see,' she said, and stretched her hands out in
case he was offering a glass but missing her direction as
her fingers came into contact with his bare forearm.

Before she could move her hand away his hand had
imprisoned it and he was turning her hand, placing a
glass of something in it and guiding it back to her mouth.
He waited while she swallowed the contents, then he was
taking the glass from her and was back again, his hands on
her arms half lifting her from the chair.

'It's bed for you,' he said matter-of-factly, and only half aware what was going on, feeling completely disorientated, she felt his hands at her clothes.

Violently she jerked away, almost passing out as pain rocked her and she was glad then to hang on to him as he steadied her and instructed her to step out of her trousers. When her briefs slid down with her trousers the pain in her head was so bad she could do no more than make a half-hearted attempt to retrieve them. Then agony was shooting through her blotting out any inbuilt instinct she had for modesty, and she just had to cling on to him.

Sensitive to all noise, a change in his tone got through to her as, her arms around his neck as he lifted her into the bed she heard him mutter a tight, 'You smell warm and sweet.' Cool sheets were about her when he ground out something about how one's senses can be deceiving, and then as pain took full possession, the last thing she heard before he left the room was the sound of the curtains being pulled to.

At what stage the attack lessened permitting her to fall asleep, Aldona didn't know. But she had a feeling she hadn't slept very long. She opened her eyes and thought for a moment that her vision had not returned. Then as her eyes became accustomed to the darkness she was able to make out shades of light and dark in the room, the lighter shade coming from the direction of the window.

Her head still muzzy, but nowhere near as violently aching as it had been, she pushed the covers back intending to get out of bed, then gasped, appalled. She was stark naked.

Searing hot colour seemed to reach every part of her as she recalled piece by piece as if in slow motion, everything that had happened before she had given way to the attack. Zeb had undressed her! And she had let him!

She left the curtains drawn to as she groped her way

to the bathroom and from the light outside found a robe
hanging behind the door. Not wanting to be found naked if
Zeb returned, she hastily put it on. Then returning to the
bedroom she flicked on the main light and saw the clothes
she had worn had been placed in a pile on one of the two
chairs.

Her intention to get dressed was thwarted by a woozy
feeling that came over her and she sat down trying to get
some clear idea of what to do for the best. She couldn't
stay here dressed as she was, yet she didn't think she had
the energy to get dressed in a dinner gown and go downstairs. Her eyes caught sight of her watch on a table beside
the bed and she left the chair to find it had gone eleven.
The matter seemed decided for her. It was probably too
late for dinner anyway now—not that she wanted any. But
by the time she was washed and dressed she would almost
certainly bump into Zeb, if he hadn't arrived before she
left. That thought alone was sufficient to have her picking
up the clothes she had been wearing when the migraine
had struck.

She hesitated. What was the point? She could just see
Zeb's face when he returned to find her sitting there
dressed in her trousers and shirt, just hear his cynical
sarcasm. He might even take it into his head to undress
her again.

She wanted badly to flee, not to be there when he came
back, but knew her time for running was over and her
eyes darted around looking for her case. She couldn't see
it until she raised her eyes to the space at the top of the
wardrobe, and saw Zeb must have hefted it up there out
of the way. She grabbed hold of the handle, aware of the
thud it made as it hit the wardrobe on the way down. Then
with a sense of urgency upon her she quickly extracted
her cotton nightdress, then as quickly closed her case and

pushed it back to the place Zeb had put it. In the bathroom she rinsed her face, then got into her nightdress.

If she had to lie beside him tonight then she intended to have something covering her. At the back of her mind she knew she was hoping to be asleep when he returned, was praying hard that he would think she was still beset by that agonising pain. For she was remembering the way he had been gentle with her. He had taken prompt action to get her into bed once he knew she couldn't see. Not once had his fingers lingered on her. And she just knew she would not have fared so well had it been Lionel Downs who had put her to bed.

Her thoughts as she climbed into bed seemed to be a mass of fear, hope, and broken sentences with not one having been completed. Then just as she lay down and pulled the covers over her the full extent of what a quagmire her mind was hit her—probably the aftermath of migraine, she thought, but she had forgotten to turn off the light switch by the door. About to get out of bed, she heard a key in the door, and with her eyes growing wide, all thoughts of feigning sleep going from her as a trembling began somewhere inside, she stared as though like a hypnotised wild animal as Zeb came through the door, closed it, then came over to the bed to look down at her.

He was wearing a lightweight lounge suit of a pale grey, though she had no remembrance of hearing him change out of the casual clothes he had been wearing the last time she had seen him. And he seemed to have taken on giant proportions as he bent over to give her face a thorough scrutiny. Whether he was satisfied with what he saw she didn't know, for she had the covers up to her chin and there wasn't very much of her visible.

'How's the head?' he asked, his grey eyes seeming to

penetrate right to the centre of her being.

It was because he asked her in a quiet voice as though he was genuinely concerned, with not a trace of cynicism there, or so she thought, that she forgot entirely her intention to hang on to the pretence of still having a migraine for as long as she could, and found herself, to her confusion, answering him honestly.

'Much better, thank you,' she said, and immediately realised what she had said. She bit her lip. Oh dear, she was helpless at deception. She felt the bed go down as Zeb sat on the side of it.

'Your full vision has returned?'

'Yes.'

'Good. Then we shan't need the services of the hotel doctor.'

'Doctor?' The brown eyes that hadn't been able to hold his penetrating stare jumped back to him in surprise.

'I've just been having a word with the hotel doctor,' he said as if it was by the way. 'He tells me that though there's nothing can be done to stop a migraine attack once it's underway, there's an injection that might help. However,' he added, making to rise, 'since you appear to be fully recovered ...'

'My head's still muzzy,' she said quickly, putting in a late claim to be an invalid who shouldn't be touched.

She knew then as he changed his mind about getting up from the bed, and stayed sitting, his eyes once more going over her face, that Zeb was up to every trick in the book. Only it wasn't a trick, her head *was* still muzzy. If he had noted as she had in the dressing table mirror that her eyes were dark from the pain she had experienced, he didn't remark upon it, but stood up.

'We'd better see about having some food sent up for you,' he said, going over to the telephone.

'I couldn't eat a thing,' said Aldona, 'honestly.' She was surprised he had remembered she had missed her dinner. But he looked back at her, then taking her at her word he came away from the phone going to switch on a small table lamp by the side of the bed away from where she lay. He went over and snicked off the centre light. She watched as his hand reached up as he undid the knot in his tie taking it off and dropping it over the back of a chair. When his hands went to the buttons on his shirt, she closed her eyes.

She kept her eyes closed until she felt the depression on the other side of the bed that told her she had company. And the trembling that had started again from the moment his tie had come off, which could have been anything from five minutes to an hour for all she knew so agitated had she become, had taken over so completely that she knew he must soon be aware of it.

She felt his body near, though not touching. He had left the lamp on, she knew, but she wasn't opening her eyes. That was until his hand came across and touched the shoulder furthest from him. Then her eyes shot open to see he was half leaning across her, the covers partly away from her to just below her shoulders. But it was those dark grey eyes that had her swallowing. She could feel the dry warmth of his hand through her nightdress, and that alone was sufficient to have her breath coming in painful gasps.

'What's this?' he asked, fingering the material. 'I don't recall covering your delectable shape in anything so demure as this little item.'

Aldona thanked the shadows in the softly lit room for concealing the blush that covered her at his reference to seeing her naked.

'I-I—don't—like t-to—sleep w-without anything on,'

she got out, stuttering like a faulty valve.

'I do,' he said smoothly, his meaning obvious. Oh dear, he hasn't got a stitch on, she thought, and knew he wasn't lying. 'Is your trembling an after-feature of migraine?' he asked, his fingers finding their way beneath the cotton material covering her shoulder. His touch slow and caressing, did nothing to calm her.

'I ... I ...' she began helplessly, then didn't have time to say any more, because she was too busy battling with the panic that was threatening to swamp her as he undid the small bow, low at the neck of her nightdress, and was pushing that material to one side his fingers seeking the curving swell of her breast, whether by accident or design passing lingeringly over the sensitive tip. And then his face was coming nearer to her. She pulled her hand back, shaken when as she brought it up automatically to push him away it came into contact with his bare chest.

'Please!' she choked, when his mouth was only inches away from her own, then in a low moan that came from the heart, 'Oh Zeb—please don't!' she cried huskily.

He pulled back from her, his eyes again studying her face. Her eyes had a shimmer of tears in them, and he could be forgiven for thinking they were tears of pain. At any rate his one hand ceased caressing her and went back to her shoulder, his grip crushing as he controlled his desire. Aldona thought she heard him call himself a name as though he didn't like himself very much, but whether it was because his better nature was having him listening to her plea, or whether it was because she was thwarting his attempt to possess her, she didn't know. It could have been because he had started anything at all when she had already told him she had a muzzy head, but she didn't know enough about him to know.

But she did know, with a rush of relief that eased her

breathing as his hands moved from her, that he was not
going to make love to her until she was fully recovered.

'Sleep well, Aldona,' he said, his voice sardonic. 'I'm
sure it won't interfere with your sleep if I tell you I always
wake early.' She closed her eyes at the taunt. 'Perhaps,
like me, you find making love in the morning gets the day
off to a very pleasant start.' She heard the lamp snick off
and opened her eyes in the darkness as he moved and
presented her with his back. 'Pleasant dreams, *sweetie*,' he
said over his shoulder.

Dreams were far away as she lay there listening to his
breathing change gradually to a deep steady rhythm that
told her he was asleep. She was wide awake, and it was
a *nightmare*. The nasty way he had called her 'sweetie'
reminded her he had overheard Lionel Downs call her by
that name, and had her thoughts in an uproar. But it
wasn't only that that had sleep light years away. Apart from
the fact that she just couldn't relax with Zeb lying sleep-
ing beside her, his reference to the fact that when he
awoke she would be earning the three thousand he had
paid, it was the fact that that tingling sensation had
started up inside her again the moment he had begun to
touch her. Panic-stricken as she had been at what she
thought would happen, through that terror had come that
disturbing awareness of him. That unwanted sensation that
told her that once he put his experience to work, once his
firm lips had taken hers, that once he progressed from
there he might well arouse the feeling he had awakened in
her when he had kissed her down on the beach—that
feeling of wanting him to kiss her. And lying awake in
the darkness, she knew then that that was something she
just couldn't take. Bravely she faced the facts as she knew
them. She had come here prepared to sell herself in order
to save her father. What she was doing was alien to every-

thing that was in her. But going against everything her high-moralled father had taught was just something that had to be done, had had the saving grace that in doing so she would be punishing herself to meet the demands required of her. She needed that punishment in order to be able to live with herself afterwards. But how could she live with herself if in selling herself for money, at the end of Zeb's lovemaking, she actually found she had *enjoyed* it!

She knew enough about herself to know there would be no living with herself if that happened. The night sped on as she tried to analyse her thoughts. Thoughts of how to save her father she had thought she could detach herself from the situation and go through with it were at rebellion with the fear mingled with the remembered thrill of pleasure she had experienced when Zeb had touched her breast. And as the thought came and refused to be shaken off that since it was clear Lionel Downs and Zeb hated each other, and that therefore if she tried to get away she could be sure Lionel wouldn't tell him where he could find her or aid him in any way if he came looking for her, she knew, underhand though it would be, she was just going to have to try it.

She picked up her watch from the table beside her, heard the metallic click and kept her breathing even lest she had disturbed her bed companion. Then when the tenor of Zeb's breathing remained unchanged, she stealthily strapped her watch to her wrist, then very carefully got out of bed. Once on her feet she was unsure what to do, then recalling the thud her suitcase had made when she had pulled it down before, she decided there was nothing for it but she would have to leave it behind. Her passport was in her handbag down by the chair where her trousers and shirt were. Thank goodness she had thought to bring

her savings with her; she might need all of them for her air
fare. Like a thief in the night she tiptoed over to the chair
that housed her clothes, then making sure she had every
item, she bundled them up in her arms, found her handbag without too much trouble, then took a few deep
breaths as she prepared herself for the hardest part—that
part of getting through the door without disturbing the
man in the bed. For if he discovered what she was up
to, she just knew there would be no waiting for dawn to
break before she was made to start paying off her debt.

Aldona was sweating profusely by the time she made
it into the corridor outside and had noiselessly closed the
door behind her. Then, her breathing easier, she was off
up the corridor in her nightdress, and into one of the
bathrooms at the end, having a strip-wash before dressing and stuffing her nightdress in her bag. Then with
the assumed air of a millionairess who thought it was perfectly reasonable to ask Reception to get her a taxi to the
airport in the middle of the night, she was taking her
first steps to putting an end to the enterprise that had
threatened to make her a physical and mental wreck.

CHAPTER FIVE

ALDONA had been back in her flat a good ten minutes
before she dared give her first sigh of relief, and it was
another hour before the tensions that had held her in their
grip let go, and she was able to realise she had really pulled
it off.

She recalled the interminable wait she had had at Luqa
Airport, expecting at every second to see Zeb come and
haul her back to the hotel with the casual comment to

anyone watching, 'My merchandise'. It had been nine
o'clock before her plane had taken off. Zeb had told her
he was an early riser, and that had done nothing to quiet
her fears. Her every hope had been pinned on the thought
that when he awoke and found her gone, he would assume,
seeing that her suitcase was still there, that she was an
early riser too. He had evidence of that since she had been
on the beach before him yesterday. Perhaps he had gone
to the beach looking for her. Perhaps he had searched
further afield. So long as it kept him from finding out she
had done a flit, she didn't much care where he went.

During the afternoon she rang Mrs Armstrong at the
nursery and told her her plans had changed and if required she could come in to work the next day.

'Oh, would you, Aldona? Wendy is still off sick and
I could do with you,' said Mrs Armstrong, obviously very
keen to have her report for duty.

Aldona queried her starting time and when asked if
she could manage the seven-thirty shift, she agreed that
she would be there and hung up, musing that Mrs Armstrong had not questioned why she was ready to go to
work after only one day off of her holiday. Then recalling
the look Mrs Armstrong had given to her left hand when
she had asked for the time off, she realised Mrs Armstrong was being rather tactful by not alluding to it.

She wondered what to do about her father. She hated
lying to him, but had already done so by telling him she was
going to stay with Hilary. She realised that at the end
of two weeks she would have to go and see him and answer
falsely all his questions on how Hilary and the baby were,
and invent things she had done during her stay, so she
went and telephoned her old home, only to hear from
Barbara that her father was in the bath.

Barbara was not sounding as cool towards her as she

had done, Aldona thought, musing that perhaps their mutual concern over her father's health on her previous phone call must have broken the ice.

'Any message I can give him?' Barbara asked.

'I changed my mind about going to Hilary's,' she answered, knowing Barbara would relate their conversation to her father. 'One of the assistants at the nursery has gone off sick leaving us short-handed.' Well, that was only half a lie; Wendy was sick, but had been off work before Aldona had asked for the time off. 'So I decided to stay and help out. I can always go to Hilary's later.'

'Will you be here on Wednesday as usual?' Barbara asked.

'Er—would you mind if I changed the night to Tuesday?' she asked in reply, and was relieved as well as pleasantly surprised when Barbara didn't ask if there was any special reason why Wednesday was out, but said instead:

'Tuesday will be fine. I shall be in myself,' then a pause as if she was taking a deep breath. 'It's about time we got to know one another, Aldona.'

Aldona returned to her attic flat, feeling a happiness inside her that had been sadly missing of late. Barbara hadn't sounded at all aloof or offputting. She had in actual fact sounded as though she regretted that they weren't closer, and though sensitive to being snubbed Barbara had been brave enough to be the first to offer the hand of friendship. Aldona knew she was going to grasp that hand. As Barbara had said, it was about time they got to know one another.

The next night found her ringing the doorbell of her old home and waiting politely on the other side of the door until someone came to answer it. It was Barbara who pulled back the door, and on seeing her stepdaughter standing there, greeted her:

'Hello. Did you forget your key?' She stood back to allow her over the threshold.

'I'm—I'm never sure,' Aldona said hesitatingly, as she stepped into the hall, 'how you feel about me just walking in.'

The two of them stopped, Barbara looking at her solemnly before a slow smile lit her face. 'I'd like you always to think of this as your home,' she said tentatively. 'Please use your door key in future, Aldona.'

For a moment Aldona wasn't sure what to say. And then as she looked at the woman who had married her father, was making him happy, for all she might have expensive tastes, she felt a glow of warmth begin to spread inside, and she leaned forward and for the first time kissed Barbara's cheek.

'Thank you,' she said simply, and knew she had done the right thing when Barbara's smile fairly beamed back at her.

'Come on through,' she invited. 'Roland has been looking forward to your visit since I told him you were coming.'

Her father stood up as she entered the room, and straightaway she noticed the difference in him. He looked so well as to be blooming with health, and she just knew, whether the outside auditors were in or not, he just didn't have a care in the world.

'You're looking well,' she said brightly, wondering again, as a rush of love for him came over her, how she could have thought for one minute in that blackest of moments that she would let him die rather than have to go through with her agreement with Lionel Downs.

'I am well,' he told her, his eyes checking her face to see how she was. 'Are you eating enough? You look thinner than when you lived at home.'

She had in fact shed seven pounds since last Wednesday, but that didn't surprise her, but now with all that behind her she had no doubts she would soon put it back on again.

'Of course I'm eating enough,' she said, and teased him, 'And you used to say *I* was a fusspot!'

The next twenty minutes were spent in general conversation, until it came to Aldona that with Guy back at work now, for all she was fairly confident he wouldn't have mentioned their broken engagement voluntarily, if her father had made some remark to him about her, then he could well have intimated that all was not as it should be between them.

She looked at the man who singlehanded had guided her through her childhood, coped proudly, scorning outside help, and her love for him welled up as she saw him looking so well and happy. A love that didn't have to seek to forgive him his one lapse that could have resulted in her bearing a permanent scar. Forgiveness didn't have to be thought of when you loved someone, it came automatically.

'Dad,' she said, and turned to look at Barbara so she would know she was included, 'I've—er—I'm no longer engaged to Guy.' It had come out more bluntly than she had intended, but there really hadn't been any way to dress it up.

She saw a look pass between him and Barbara and hoped that didn't mean that he was upset and looking at her stepmother for assistance. But he didn't look at all upset when he turned his attention back to her and said quietly:

'I know.'

'You know!' She hadn't thought Guy would have told him, but he must have done.

'Lionel Downs told me you'd broken your engagement

when he came back from giving you a lift last Wednesday.'

Oh, how could he! She'd particularly asked him not to.
She felt a flare of anger surge up inside her against Lionel
Downs. Aside from the fact he had risked upsetting her
father more than he had been, the news must have made
him feel a bit aggrieved that she hadn't been the one to
tell him. And then her anger died as she realised Lionel
must have told him *after* he had given her father his
cheque for two thousand pounds. Barbara had said he had
been his old self when she had come home, so her broken
engagement would hardly have impinged on his consciousness, what with the relief at having the money drown-
ing all other thoughts. All the same, she couldn't help but
feel a shade awkward that she hadn't been the one to tell
him.

'I—meant to tell you myself,' she said, and invented,
'only with Lionel Downs here I couldn't very well. Then
on the way home he—er—noticed I wasn't wearing my
engagement ring.' She thought she'd be labouring the
point if she tried to invent anything to add to that, then
knowing how he had always liked Guy, she asked, 'You
don't mind, do you? Only ...' and got another surprise as
her father broke in:

'He wasn't the right man for you.'

'Wasn't the right man!' Aldona gasped. 'But I thought
you liked him?'

'He ...' Roland Mayhew began, looked at Barbara again,
then appeared to be on the point of telling her exactly
what it was he didn't like about her ex-fiancé. Though that
would have been new coming from her father. She had
never heard him run anyone down, it just wasn't his way
to speak ill of anyone. He didn't now, though she was sure
when he merely repeated, 'He wasn't the right man for

you,' that that wasn't what he had started out to say. 'You're much too good for him,' he added, with a father's overstatement.

The rest of the evening passed off happily, and with Barbara welcoming her every comment, Aldona felt really wanted in the relaxed threesome—to the extent that when the time came for her to leave, she had long lost any feeling of awkwardness with her, and was feeling well on the way to having a new friend.

The remainder of the week followed its normal course, with her going to work and finishing early to come back to her flat to relax, reading or sewing or whatever came to hand. Guy had been her companion on most of her outings recently, but though she still had friends in her old set, she wasn't in any rush to get back into the swing again. She was still feeling a little bruised from her experience in Malta. Zeb popped into her mind too often for comfort, causing her to have several inward battles in trying to oust him. Even a week later her stomach still churned over when she imagined his fury when he had awakened and found she had left.

At the end of the next week, remembrances of Malta were growing dimmer, though it was strange, she thought, how easily she could remember every feature of Zeb's face. Well, you wouldn't forget, would you? she told herself; after all, she owed him three thousand pounds. You couldn't have had the upbringing she had had for that remembrance and the face of the man she had cheated not to come back time and time again.

It was on the Sunday, almost two weeks since her hasty exit from Malta, that around six o'clock a knock on her door had her going to answer it—and that sick feeling she had hoped never to feel again began gnawing at her insides when she saw her caller was Lionel Downs.

Someone must have left the front door open for him to find his way up to her flat. He was puffing from climbing the stairs and she smelt alcohol on his breath. From his disgruntled expression she could see that his visit meant nothing agreeable for her, and though she couldn't remember when anything to do with him had ever been agreeable, she didn't want any of her neighbours coming in or going out overhearing anything of what he had to say.

Unspeaking, she stood back from the door, inviting him in and closing the door after him, but standing near to it as she waited for him to tell her the purpose of his call.

He didn't keep her waiting very long but started straightaway to enlighten her. 'You owe me, girlie,' he told her bluntly, and while her stomach flipped as she thought, Oh no, not that again, he went on. 'Those cheques you gave me weren't met.'

'Weren't met?' Oh *no*! Zeb had told her he was not a poor man, and his clothes had borne that out. She just hadn't given a thought to the fact that anyone with a cheque book could write cheques to the value of three thousand pounds, but that didn't necessarily mean that they had three thousand pounds in the bank. But she found it too incredible to grasp that that must in fact be what Zeb had done.

'You mean——' she said hoarsely, the full realisation of what it meant hitting her, 'You mean he didn't have three thousand pounds in the bank?'

'He's got more money than he'll ever need,' said Lionel Downs, his belligerency at being done out of his money evident. 'It isn't that the money isn't there,' he added. 'He just decided to instruct his bank to stop payment.'

Aldona felt as though she had been kicked in the stomach. This was something she hadn't given a thought to. She should have done, that much was obvious, but she just hadn't. Had she really thought, though, that she could just take his money and run? That he would let her get away with it? She had gone pale, and knew Lionel Downs had witnessed it. He knew he had her scared, but he was making no allowances for it as he told her:

'I want my money back, or ...' No, she thought, oh no! She knew what was coming, but she couldn't go through all that again, she just couldn't. But it wasn't her body Lionel Downs was after this time, she found, as he continued with a snarl in his voice as he witnessed from her expression that the thought of going to bed with him was making her feel ill. 'You can stick your favours, Miss Hoity-Toity Mayhew, I've got other fish to fry. But unless I get my money by tomorrow, your father will find he's got quite a lot of explaining to do to the auditors.'

The relief she felt that she didn't have to give herself to this horrible man was shortlived as fresh fright took over that her father's health was still threatened. He's bluffing, she thought, trying to stay calm as a shifty look came over him. And from somewhere, heaven knew where, she found a spark of courage to call his bluff.

'You gave me to understand in Malta that my father was in the clear. He would have banked that cheque you gave him at the first opportunity,' she said, her calm wavering that this most objectionable man was far more cunning than she ever would be. 'You have ...' her voice broke, 'you have nothing on him.'

'I'm not an accountant for nothing,' he told her, his voice loaded with meaning.

'You mean you'd ...'

'Try my culinary expertise on the books?' he interrupted her. 'You're damned right I would! I'm missing three thousand, either you cough up—in cash this time or your old man is for the high jump.'

'But—but——' Aldona was floundering in a vortex of

despair. Lionel had her exactly where he wanted her, ready to grovel, and she could see it pleased him mightily that there was nothing hoity-toity about her now. 'Tomorrow's too soon,' she said, desperately playing for time. 'I might be able to get you the money. B—But not by tomorrow.' Oh, the crazy things one said when one was frightened out of one's wits! If there had been the remotest chance of her getting even the two thousand did Lionel Downs think she would ever have gone off with him in the first place?

She saw his eyes light up like a cash register at her intimation that there was a chance the money might be forthcoming.

'All right, girlie, perhaps I am pushing it a bit for you to find yourself another sucker to sell yourself to. I'll give you till midnight on Tuesday. I'll give you my home number—it's ex-directory—and when you have the money just ring through.' Aldona followed the farce through, finding a piece of paper and a pencil for him to write his number down, knowing those digits would never be dialled. 'If I don't happen to answer the phone,' he concluded, moving his bulk towards the door, 'you can leave a message to say there's a parcel ready for me to collect.' His smile was just about the most awful thing she had ever seen as he opened the door and said, 'Don't forget, girlie, three thousand cash by midnight Tuesday or your old man has had it.'

In the twenty-four hours following his visit, Aldona had frozen up within herself. She had gone to work on Monday and not even the quaint remarks of the children could thaw her. From habit she coped with her work, forcing a smile for the children's benefit, but her heart wasn't in it.

Back at her flat she paced up and down the way she had done when this whole wretched business had begun, but her mind hit a brick wall every time she tried to find a way out of this second crisis. Her mind went over the same territory it had gone over that hideous Wednesday nearly three weeks ago, but with an even worse result. This time there wasn't anybody blackmailing her to sell herself to them. Lionel Downs had other fish to fry, he had said. Well, good luck to her, whoever she was. But oh, what could she do?

She gave full consideration to trying to contact Sebastian Thackeray. Lionel Downs had said he was abroad, but that had been over two weeks ago. Surely by now he was back. But what did she tell him if she did manage to track him down? That his chief internal auditor had given her father two thousand pounds and that unless she paid him back three thousand pounds then he was going to cook the books to show her father up for the thief he was? She winced at the word; she still couldn't credit that her father who valued honour above most things could have done such a thing. Then because she had the evidence of how ill he had looked and how he had rapidly improved after Lionel Downs had given him that cheque, there was no disbelieving it. She turned her thoughts back to Sebastian Thackeray. He was probably an old man with the same high morals she had accredited to her father. Whatever she told him, it would still come down to her father being dismissed, and prosecuted. And though she wouldn't mind at all Lionel Downs being hauled over the coals for his part in it, it was going to be her father who would suffer the stress and anxiety of waiting for a court case that would in all probability kill him.

As the hands of her watch neared seven o'clock that night, Aldona knew there was nothing for it but that she would have to go and see her father. She must at least give him some warning that there was trouble ahead. That meant, of course, she would have to tell him she knew a little of what he had done. Though it had come to her that he would probably have a heart attack on the spot if she told him what she had been up to. Whatever happened he mustn't know about that Malta trip; she could picture his horror now that after his careful instruction in her adolescence, in order to save him she had gone with Lionel Downs prepared to be his mistress. She would have to make out that Lionel had let something slip that night he had brought her home, that it had played on her mind, and that last night she had rung him to find out more— or something . . .

Having no clear idea just which way she would approach her father, she set off knowing only that he and Barbara would be surprised to see her since she had said her night for visiting them would in future be Tuesdays. Though for all there would be no keeping it from Barbara, she was hoping to have some time alone with her father. Perhaps if she didn't offer to help make the coffee as she had done last Tuesday . . .

As Barbara had invited, Aldona let herself in when she reached the house, and feeling as though she had just come out from a Turkish bath, she approached the sitting room door. And there she stopped, all her senses shouting alarm as she heard the sound of two definitely male voices, their words muffled, coming from within. Terrified lest it was Lionel Downs with her father, screaming fear uppermost that he was telling him she had gone away with him—he wouldn't be telling him about the money until he was sure he wasn't going to get it—she had a lightning vision of her father becoming incensed and straining his already weakened heart by setting about him.

In a flash she was in the room, the propulsion of her energetic entrance taking her into the centre of the room, her jaw dropping open as she tried to hide first the dis-belief, and secondly the panic, that the man with her father was not Lionel Downs but a man who was twenty years or more younger. A man she had never expected to see again. A man whose only name she knew was Zeb.

'It's not Tuesday, is it, Aldona?' Roland Mayhew teased, having broken off his conversation with his guest when she had burst into the room, unperturbed by her sudden entrance though looking as though he might tease her about it later. Then, observing the way she was staring at the tall athletic-looking man who had been seated, but had stood up when she had come in, 'This is my daughter, Mr ...' he started, only to find no introduction necessary as Zeb cut in smoothly:

'We've met.'

Aldona nearly died. She was half turned from her father, who was exclaiming, 'You've met!' just as though he thought him well out of her orbit, she thought, her mind having seized up, her wide brown eyes horror-struck, dread about her that he was going to reveal the circumstances of their meeting.

She saw the very devil was in his eyes as he coolly looked back, those dark grey eyes telling her nothing other than that he couldn't see why he should keep quiet after what she had done.

'It was ...' He paused, deliberately, she thought, as sweat broke out on her brow, 'at the Nightingales' party, wasn't it, Aldona?'

If he'd said King Kong's party, she'd have agreed. 'Y-yes, that's right,' she said, knowing he was all set to make her hair stand on end with fright at every half-said sentence, but willing to suffer it all as long as he didn't give her away.

'How are you?' he asked, with the politeness one might

use to a person met casually at a party. 'You managed to get home without too much difficulty, I trust?'

'I took a taxi,' she gabbled quickly, hoping her father was thinking her escort at the Nightingales' had succumbed to drink or something and hadn't been fit to drive.

'I would have brought you home had you told me you wanted to go,' said Zeb, proving to her father what a perfect gentleman he was, she thought sourly. 'It was a surprise to see you there one minute and then to have my eyes opened to the fact that you weren't.'

That would be when he woke up, of course, she thought, glad to know she was at least thinking at last. For her brain had gone into temporary hibernation from the moment of seeing him there. Then suddenly she knew she just couldn't stay here and fend off his two-edged remarks. Her father who knew her better than anyone would soon realise there was something wrong. And just as suddenly she knew, since Zeb had been playing this game with her, that he wasn't going to give her away. That though she might begin to have doubts about that when she left them, it would only be doubt brought on by her feelings of guilt.

Her father was just telling her that Barbara had gone to visit a sick friend, going on to offer them both a drink, when Aldona refused, saying, 'This is only a flying visit,' and making it up as she went along, 'I have a dinner date at nine. I only popped in for some gloves I particularly wanted to wear.' She knew she was getting deeper into a quagmire, as she said, 'I thought I'd left my gloves here,' she could have phoned and asked, 'only they're not on the hall table, so I must have left them somewhere else.'

'You're not going out with Guy?' her father asked sharply.

'Guy?' she exclaimed, startled by his tone out of the

panic of her thoughts and realising with a sense of shock that he had really meant it when he had said Guy wasn't good enough for her. 'No-no, not Guy,' she reassured him. Colour rushed to her cheeks as she flicked her eyes in Zeb's direction and met his look full on. He was giving her a humourless look she interpreted as, 'And how much is it going to cost this one?' before she managed to drag her gaze away and say weakly to her father, 'It's someone else.' Then, 'I must dash or I'm going to be late.'

She said a quick goodbye to him and, her lips politely curving, gave Zeb a brief goodbye, and was out of the house as if a pack of hounds were after her. She was forced to stop at the gate and open it, and she paused there, noting what she hadn't noticed before, her thoughts too busily occupied elsewhere when she'd arrived, that there was a sleek opulent car pulled up outside. Lionel Downs telling her Zeb had more money than he would want came back to her, and she had no trouble in naming the car's owner.

She hadn't gone very far when she became aware that a virtually silent car was being driven slowly beside her. She had no trouble in recognising the car as the one that had stood outside her father's house, and knowing herself defeated, she stopped walking. The car stopped too, the passenger door being pushed open from the inside. The invitation to get in had been inevitable, she realised. Inevitable too was the knowledge that Zeb wanted some sort of explanation from her. She might just as well get in. He hadn't been to the trouble to trace her for her to think that by walking on it would be an end to it. Though how he had managed to find her she couldn't begin to think, for she was sure Lionel Downs wouldn't have assisted him in any away, and she was equally sure she had left no clue behind.

All the same, she hesitated about voluntarily getting in that car beside him. Then the thought came that if she didn't, he was certain to get out and take her to task on the pavement. And really, the kind of conversation she envisaged them having, with all the sordid details being aired in the street, was something she would prefer not to have any passer-by overhearing. She took the two paces required and got into the car, the smell of genuine leather greeting her. She said not a word. Zeb said nothing either until he had leaned over and pulled her door to. A feeling of claustrophobia briefly visited her, but it didn't have time to linger as he remarked, sounding as though he didn't believe she had a date at nine and had seen through her attempt to get away and so avoid any sort of confrontation with him:

'I'm sure your date won't mind waiting for you. But you'll agree, I know, that we really should have a chat.'

'I don't have a date,' she said, and wished she hadn't confirmed what he already knew. But her nerves were getting to her; a chat with him the last thing she wanted.

'Not even with this Guy your father seems to think so highly of,' was the sarcastic rejoinder, letting her know he had witnessed her father's disapproval of the man.

'I no longer see Guy,' she said woodenly, beginning to get annoyed that he was deliberately holding back on what she was sure he was intending to fell her with—her hurried flight away from him. She was sure he was working on getting her mind completely away from it, and then when she was unsuspecting—wham!—would hit her with it and so surprise her into being more honest with him than she would be if he tackled her straight away. But she wasn't so dim that she wasn't going to watch every word she said. If this was the way he was going to play it, let him. She'd be ready for him when he got to the crux of why he wanted this *chat*.

'Ran out of funds, did he?'

For a moment she had no idea what he was talking about, and then as it dawned on her that he thought she no longer went out with Guy because she had rooked him for every penny, her mouth firmed as she swallowed down her anger.

'As a matter of fact, no,' she said tightly.

'You mean you let him go *before* the kitty was empty?'

Did she really deserve this? she wondered, then with an honesty she didn't want, she faced that to Zeb, from what he knew of her, she probably did.

'We were engaged,' she explained. Why she had told him that she couldn't think, unless it was that part of her didn't want the conversation to continue this way. Perhaps it was a feeling of wanting him to believe she was not really as bad as she must seem, that there might be something more to her than grab all she could, if she could get him to see she had thought herself in love, and as a consequence got herself engaged. But he didn't see anything of the sort in what she had said.

'What happened?' he ground out. 'Did he find you in bed with a man old enough to be your grandfather?'

Aldona stifled a gasp. He knew how to hurt. But there was something else in his voice aside from the jibe and it had her recalling again those raised voices she had heard in that room in Malta. Had his remark, 'I'll get you out or die in the attempt', meant that Lionel Downs had been playing around with a girl-friend of his and he wanted to get her away from him? She couldn't see it. What girl in her right mind would choose Lionel Downs when Zeb was around? But his jibe had stung, and in an attempt at bravado words were leaving her, careless that they might find a sore spot.

'What's the matter?' she jibed in return. 'Have you some down on wealthy old men?'

'Your homework's at fault,' he jeered.

'Homework?' she queried.

'Who told you Downs was wealthy?'

Apart from being glad Lionel had two thousand pounds to spare to help her father, she knew nothing of the state of his finances. But she remembered now the look of greed in his eyes when she had handed him the cheques for three thousand pounds. The fact that he was dunning her now for not only the return of his money, but an extra thousand, showed he was avaricious.

She became aware Zeb was looking at her as though waiting for an answer to his question, and her attempt at bravado disappeared as nausea attacked her. She had had a fairly sheltered upbringing and to be tossed into the deep end, of having a seamy side of life brought home to her— and, it had to be faced, being a part of that seamy side— was like having dirt she was powerless to wash off clinging to her.

Needing an urgent change of subject if her stomach was to behave, she opened her mouth intending to ask the question of how had Zeb found her father, when he sent her temper rocketing by not waiting any longer for her answer to his question, and told her she had backed a loser if she thought Lionel Downs was the owner of a gravy train, and going on to say:

'But perhaps you realised that in Malta. You dropped him soon enough when I told you I wasn't a poor man, didn't you?' His cool had vanished from him at that point as he bit into her. 'You lost no time in finding out the number of my room and making the journey up to the next floor, did you?'

'I didn't know it was your room,' she inserted hotly.

'Like hell you didn't!' he snarled, before she could tell him she had no idea then which floor she had been on.

'You put on a good act, I'll grant you that. Timed asking for three thousand just right, didn't you, you little cheat?'

'Cheat?' she echoed.

'That's what I said—cheat,' he repeated. 'Wouldn't you say it was cheating to take money for services rendered, and then not render those services?'

Nausea fled, as her temper snapped. 'Me a cheat!' she gasped. 'And what do you think you are?' She was too angry then to reason that it was she who had cancelled their contract by running out on him the way she had. 'You lost no time in cancelling those cheques, did you? You know as well as I that—that . . .'

Her voice tailed off as Zeb gave her a look of such fierce fury she thought he was going to hit her. He did grab hold of her arms, his fingers biting into her, causing her temper to flee as fear made itself felt. What had she said, for heaven's sake, to make him look like that? Then as he held her in his merciless grip, control seemed to come to him, and he flung her back against her seat, his hands coming away from her as though he felt besmirched by having touched her. Then with a control that amazed her after having witnessed the very real fury in him, he said coldly:

'So you've seen the delightful Lionel since he returned from his holiday?'

Aldona saw then that whatever it was between him and Lionel Downs was still there. Saw that her knowing about the cancelled cheques had told him she must have seen Lionel again, or else how could she have known? But what was confusing her more than ever was the fact that Zeb had looked furious enough to set about her when, if her theory about him wanting to get Lionel Downs away from his girl-friend was right, then why wasn't he clapping his hands that he thought she had taken up with him again?

'I have seen him since he came back,' she admitted, not seeing how she could deny it with him having so quickly reasoned that out for himself. But she was unprepared to see that fury return to his face as he spat out, his temper boiling:

'You've been to bed with him again!'

'No, I haven't,' she flared, her anger matching his at the suggestion. 'And for your information, I never did go to bed with him.'

'Like hell you never did!' he roared, and she just knew she could swear it on a stack of Bibles and he wouldn't believe her. 'Downs gave you his cheque before you went away with him, didn't he?' and not waiting for her reply, 'He'd expect full payment for his money, and I know for a fact you spent one night at least with him. There were probably other nights too before you got as far as Malta.'

'Well, at least his cheque was honoured,' she snapped, only saying that because she was in over her head and with him not prepared to believe her, resorting to trying any tactic that would get him away from what he thought had gone on between her and Lionel Downs.

'Did you honestly think I wouldn't stop payment on my cheques?' he asked. 'You're not as sharp as you would have one believe if you thought that, Miss Mayhew. I paid an exorbitant price for what you were offering, and let me tell you, no one defrauds me without me getting even.' That had an ominous ring to it that made her insides quail. But what he had to say next was so mind-blowing that for several seconds she just couldn't take it in. 'Not even,' he went on, his tone unbearably superior, 'a little trollop my *stepfather* knew first.'

At first the word 'stepfather' didn't penetrate, for all Zeb had emphasised it in a sneering tone. And Aldona was about to reiterate that she hadn't known Lionel Downs that way, when her breath went from her in one strangled gasp. And as the word 'stepfather' whirled around in her brain she gasped again, and said on a hoarse breath:

'Stepfather?' She had to swallow before adding faintly, 'Are you saying that—that Lionel Downs is your stepfather?'

CHAPTER SIX

'You didn't know?' It must be clear to him that she hadn't known, for she was staring at him in the fading light, her eyes wide with shock. 'My mother married him two years ago,' he said flatly, and she knew from that that in his opinion it was the worst day's work she had ever done. Aldona reasoned then that with Lionel Downs telling her he wasn't married, then Zeb's mother must have since died. And knowing how sad she would feel if it was her dear departed relative they were talking of, she said softly:

'I'm sorry.'

'*You're* sorry!' The words sprang from him as if her being sorry was the last thing he expected to hear, before he aloofly told her, 'My mother is not in need of your sympathy. She married Downs and seems prepared to put up with him.'

An assault of fresh shock had her gasping anew. 'Your mother's alive? You mean she's still married to him?' Her voice had risen to a high note. 'You mean she isn't—they aren't divorced,' her voice petered out as she added, 'or anything?'

'Or nothing,' he said. 'That swine and my mother are still married.'

'Oh, Zeb,' the words came from her all choked, 'I didn't

know he was married. Honestly I didn't.'

'Would it have mattered if you had?' he asked harshly.

'Of course it would,' she snapped. 'What do you take me for?'

'I thought that fact was already established,' he told her insultingly, and caught her hand as the shock she had received combined with his insult proved too much for her, and her hand swung in an arc without her instruction.

'Cut that out,' he growled, as he held her wrist to prevent her blow from landing. 'Try any of that stuff with me and you'll be giving what you promised back in Malta without being paid for it!'

That quietened her. Zeb wasn't the sort of man to use threats lightly. She reached for the door handle of the car. As far as she was concerned their 'chat' was at an end, and all she could do was to thank God she had got away from Lionel Downs when she had. He had threatened one fate—the man beside her was threatening the same one. And she just didn't trust herself, the way she was feeling right at this moment, not to take another swing at him if he again insulted her so vilely.

His hand came down over hers, taking it away from the door handle. 'Where do you think you're going?'

'Back to my flat—I can't think of another thing we have to discuss.'

'I'll take you to your flat,' he said, his tone authoritative, leaving her to guess if he too thought their discussion over.

Feeling as though she had just broken all records for the hundred yards dash, Aldona gave him her address and leaned back in her seat, exhausted. There was as much point in withholding where she lived as saying she preferred to walk. Zeb intended to drive her back to her flat, and if she didn't tell him where she lived she wouldn't put it past him to lock her in the car and go back and ask her father for her address.

Her father! She'd hardly given him a thought this last half hour. Zeb set the car in motion and was pulling away from the kerb as the enormous worries that he had freed her from for a short while zoomed in. Her father would have to be warned, she knew that. Would it be better for him to have another worry-free day tomorrow? The thought occupied her for some minutes, but with Zeb sitting coldly unspeaking next to her, she just couldn't think clearly. All that was coming through was that if Lionel Downs didn't have his money by midnight to-morrow, then her father ...

She just couldn't bear to think of the consequences, and though she had no intention of speaking to Zeb again, not even a 'Goodnight' did she intend to give him, so distraught did she become at the thought of what could happen to her father, she found herself babbling about anything that came into her head to keep the picture of her father's collapse at bay.

'What made you decide to go to Malta?' Of all the crass questions! She knew very well why he had gone. He had told her he had business there and she knew full well now his business had been with Lionel Downs. Zeb didn't answer, obviously not considering her question worthy of a reply. 'I mean,' she went on, the thought just occurring to her, 'If—well, since I now know he's married. I wouldn't have thought he would have told anyone where he was going. What made you think he'd head for Malta?'

'You're damned right he didn't leave a forwarding address,' was snapped at her. 'I wasn't even aware he was going on holiday. He chose a damned inconvenient time to go as it was.' He didn't bother explaining why it was inconvenient, and if it had anything to do with his mother, then Aldona would rather not know. 'I'd been abroad on some business,' he unbent sufficiently to explain, when she had thought he had said all he was going to. 'I arrived home late on Friday night, rang my mother on Saturday morning to hear he'd packed his bucket and spade and said he'd be back in two weeks. I was as mad as hell,' he went on. 'I was sure, since he hadn't bothered to ask his wife if she wanted a holiday too, then he was up to no good. I found out where he was going, just missed him at the airport, so chartered a plane.'

'You chartered a plane just to give him a piece of your mind?' she questioned, glad she wouldn't be around to see him when he really lost his temper. He must have been raging!

'That was part of it, but only a small part. I was sure he'd have some woman in tow, so I decided to follow him and obtain concrete evidence to give my mother so she could divorce him.'

'Divorce him?' Aldona felt faint, didn't want to hear any more. 'You mean ...' Oh *no*! If being prosecuted for fraud didn't kill her father, then to see her named in a divorce action definitely would—regardless of what it would do to her.

'You'll make a beautiful co-respondent, Aldona,' Zeb said pleasantly, and it was all she could do not to grab hold of him and beg him not to use her.

'I didn't sleep with him, I didn't,' she told him urgently. 'Please, please Zeb, believe me!'

'You were Mr and Mrs in the hotel register,' he reminded her.

'Yes—I know. But ... Oh, Zeb! It will kill my father. He has a bad heart. It will ...'

'It's a bit late in the day to remember that, isn't it?' he said roughly.

She wanted to tell him she had never forgotten it. Had it not been for her father's health, she would never in a thousand years have done what she had done. 'Please,' she said huskily, and had to battle to keep her tears back. Zeb would only think it an act and it wouldn't endear her to him. Noisily she swallowed down tears, and was about to beg him, 'Please!' again, when he appeared to relent. But she knew it wasn't because he had heard her trying to get herself under control that he said:

'Relax. I didn't tell my mother.'

'You ...' Words just wouldn't come.

'You and I, Aldona Mayhew, seem to have something in common.'

'Oh,' she said, unable to think of a thing.

'We both seem to have a parent to whom we can't bear to cause pain.'

She saw then what Lionel Downs had meant when he had said, 'You can't hurt me without hurting her.' 'So your mother doesn't know her husband went away with—someone?' she questioned, and needing to have it endorsed as relief started to rush in, 'You didn't tell her?'

'I couldn't,' Zeb said shortly, showing her a fine sensitivity he had so far kept well hidden. Though, remembering the way he had looked after her when she had migraine, Aldona thought she had seen a glimpse of it before.

Her relief paramount, she wanted to thank him for keeping quiet, though she knew it wasn't out of consideration for her. But he seemed to have done with the matter, and she knew he would have nothing very nice to send her way if she offered her thanks.

She fell silent, her mind moving on to wonder how, with his stepfather not leaving a forwarding address, he had managed to track him down. On impulse, her spirits more even after the fright he had given her, she broke the silence in the car and put the question to him. And oh, how she wished she had left well enough alone!

'That wasn't too difficult,' Zeb told her. 'Downs works as head of the internal auditing department. Outside auditors were due on the Monday following the Saturday he started his holiday—I said he'd chosen a damned inconvenient time to go away. He should have been there working in close liaison with them. Anyway, the firm hired to go through the books contacted Downs by phone on Friday and on learning he wouldn't be there when they started work, they pinned him down to telling him where he was going, should there be information they required that only he could supply.'

It seemed to Aldona that Zeb knew a tremendous amount of what went on at Sebastian Thackeray Limited, especially since she had gained a clear impression that if the two men said more that three words to each other, then it would be three too many.

'So you asked these outside auditors to give you his holiday address,' she guessed.

'That's right.'

'And they gave it to you without any argument?' She asked the question but didn't believe it, and she knew that must have been apparent in her voice when he said:

'Why shouldn't they? I'm the one who'll be paying their bill at the end of the audit.'

'You'll be ...' she began, not wanting to believe what her brain was telling her, and thinking her hair would be white if she received any more shocks. 'Are—are they working—for you?' she managed, her voice no more than a croak. Her eyes fixed on him, unable to drag her eyes away, she saw him nod before answering.

'Didn't Downs tell you he worked for me?' She was too

stunned to reply, was too busy thinking—so not only did Downs work for him, her father did too. This man who had stated 'No one defrauds me without me getting even' was her father's employer. He was the man her father had stolen two thousand pounds from. That the money had been repaid seemed neither here nor there then, as Zeb answered his own question, 'Of course he didn't tell you he works for me—you thought he was a wealthy man, didn't you?'

His jibe didn't even hurt, so bewildered was she. She still couldn't believe what he was telling her, and as he slowed the car down, his eyes scanning the houses for the number on the door to where she lived—she was incapable then of directing him, and he didn't appear to need her assistance—she just had to ask:

'I never did get to know your full name.' She had to clear her throat before her next words would come. 'What is it?'

'Sebastian Thackeray,' he supplied, and while she was nearly dropping with shock, he got out of the car and came round to open the door on the passenger side.

Struggling for some sense of normality, Aldona got out of the car and with legs feeling weak, found herself stammering, 'My—my father works for you.'

'I know,' he replied. Then with that authoritative note in his voice again that brooked no argument, 'I'll see you to your door.'

Aldona had heard the saying, 'Everything got too much for me,' and moving like an automaton with Zeb taking charge of her keys, escorting her inside the house where she had her flat, her head buzzing with one thought after another, she thought she had a good idea of what it meant. Just lately one crisis had followed crisis, and this latest one, this latest startling fact that the man she had run out on was none other than Sebastian Thackeray, the man who would have no compunction in seeing that her father had his just deserts if he ever found out what he had done, had her nerves gathering together in one jangled mass of fright.

Her mind tripping over itself with her thoughts, her feet stopped at the door of her attic flat purely as that part of her mind that didn't need guidance told her she had arrived at her destination. And as though he was aware she had been shaken rigid to find out who he was, Sebastian Thackeray inserted the most likely key from the key ring she had handed over in her stupefied state, and opened the door, following her in as her feet moved forward.

Realising belatedly that he must never know the full extent of the shock he had given her, Aldona put all her will power to use in keeping her clamouring thoughts at bay until he had gone. She looked across at him, ready to thank him for seeing her home intimating there was no need for him to linger. But as the words formed on her lips she saw he didn't look ready to go anywhere until he considered he was ready to go. She knew she would be wasting her time in even giving him the broadest of hints as she watched his cool grey eyes move around the sitting room of her small but modest apartment.

She wasn't ashamed of her small dwelling. She kept it immaculately, and though there were no signs of luxury about her she had thought she had managed to make it homely and comfortable. But as she saw his eyes narrow as they flicked over her faded but otherwise presentable three-piece suite and on to her shinily polished but nonetheless neither modern and far from antique furniture, she couldn't help but think he must be comparing it with what she thought would be the lush contents of his own home.

It came as a bit of a jolt as he swung his gaze in her

direction, to discover he hadn't been comparing her furniture with his at all. And the question he asked was one she wasn't ready for and had her mind scampering all ways to come up with an answer he would find fitted, as she realised just what had been in his mind as he had looked about him.

'What exactly,' he asked slowly, his dark grey eyes refusing to let hers go, 'did you spend the money on that Downs gave you?'

'Spend the money on?' she hedged, as one thought only refused to budge out of her head, that thought being that he just mustn't find out it had gone back into the coffers of Sebastian Thackeray Limited, and why.

'I can't think you have this sort of furniture about you out of sentimental value,' he enlightened her, going on to say, 'There's nothing wrong with your bits and pieces. In fact if you were on a tight budget I would have admired the way you've made it so—homely.'

That alone made her eyes widen slightly, that he had discerned the homeliness of her abode, when she was sure his settee would be plush velvet covered or genuine leather. She'd like to bet he never got up from his settee to hear the accompanying *g-doing* as the springs gave an exclamation of relief. But he wasn't leaving it there.

'I would have thought, apart from the rake off you got from Downs, that your other *admirers* would have been generous enough for you to have "feathered your nest" more in the style suitable to the sort of female you are.'

He was being deliberately insulting, she knew that. It was as if seeing the inside of her apartment with its modest furnishings had come as something of a surprise to him, and that before he left he intended to know more of her than she had so far allowed him to know.

'I—er——' she began, trying to get herself into the part

he thought fitted her, but having no idea of how such a female would act in such a confrontation, finding she was struggling.

'Just what did you do with the two thousand, Aldona?' he asked, not giving her time to get her thoughts together.

She half turned from him, saw her bedroom door was open a few inches. Through the small gap she could see the side of her wardrobe.

'Clothes,' she said, turning back to him and seeing his eyes go down over what he could see of her cotton shirt beneath the jacket she wore, and on down to her denim jeans. 'I don't like to visit my father in anything that looks expensive,' she lied, desperately hoping he would believe her.

As an edge of frost came to his face she saw that he had. She thought for a fleeting, ridiculous moment that a flicker of disappointment crossed his face at her answer. But that was purely her fear-impregnated senses picking up nuances that weren't there. She knew that especially as when next he spoke there was no trace of disappointment in his voice, but spine-curling scorn.

'That figures. You wouldn't want him knowing the kind of life you lead, would you?'

He let his eyes scan her flat again, and still dreadfully afraid he hadn't quite believed her—for all it would take her all her time to spend two thousand pounds on clothes, she didn't doubt the sort of women he normally went around with would spend that amount on only a few dresses—she jumped in with a question it seemed imperative now she knew who he was, that she had the answer to.

'Er—what were you doing at my father's house?' she asked, hoping to sound mildly enquiring, but hearing her question sharp and definite.

'I was looking for you,' he didn't hesitate to tell her.

'Looking for me!' Her insides were all of a tremble again. He had stated unequivocally that he wouldn't stand for anyone putting one over on him. Was he wanting retribution in full for her running out on him?

'I ...' He paused, causing her to look warily at him. He wasn't coming any nearer if it was retribution he had in mind. But she still didn't trust him, though she couldn't understand his pause. If he had been inventing the next bit he couldn't have taken longer over it, but she knew there was no invention in what he said next and that that pause had just been while he savoured the effect his words would have on her. 'I thought since I might need you for evidence at a later date that I'd better find you,' he told her coolly.

'Evidence at a later date? But—but ...' Was there no end to it? She just knew he was talking about the possibility of his mother divorcing Lionel Downs. 'But you said ...'

'I know what I said. I still have no intention of being the one to inflict the hurt my mother would suffer,' he paused again, and quietly added, 'not at this point.'

'Not at ...' Aldona found it impossible to go on and clutched at the back of a chair, her knuckles showing white as she fought to get on top of the horror that was rocking her.

'My mother is a warm and sensitive person,' he continued as though she hadn't spoken. 'She's been wearing rose-coloured spectacles about Downs for far too long in my opinion. But in my view it won't be much longer before she comes to realise he's nowhere near to being the man she thought she married.' His face took on a tight line, and she knew for the moment he was no longer with her as he said, 'The man's an insult to my dead father. What the hell she thought she saw in him God alone knows.'

'She must have loved him,' Aldona said quietly, though

privately wondering how anyone could love such a man.

'*Love!*' Zeb bit out as though the thought of that word in connection with his mother and his chief auditor offended him. 'Felt sorry for him more likely. Who knows what line he fed her. He had little enough going for him before he sampled a different sort of life and put on weight, but——' He halted, as if catching himself up on realising he was saying more to her than he had meant to. 'All that's beside the point,' he said sharply. 'If and when she comes to realise exactly the sort of man she's married, I may need to know where I can get hold of you.'

'You can't ...' Aldona began earnestly, only to find herself given a look that said he could and he would if he had to. She knew then she could plead with him until the cows came home, and all in vain.

And then the pride that had deserted her suddenly reasserted itself, and for all her insides were feeling grim, she lifted her head proudly and leaving the subject asked :

'How did you get to connect me with my father?'

'I didn't, at first,' he said, his brows drawing together at her proud look. 'All I had to go on was your name. I knew Downs wouldn't tell me more—he's too damned wily not to know why I should want to know more about you. So I put my mind to calculate where he'd met you. You could have been one of our past employees, I thought, which would prove less time-consuming if you were than in doing a round of the many dives he frequents, if you'd met him that way. So first I checked with Personnel, to find that the only Mayhew we had record of was a certain Roland Mayhew who's been working for us for six months or so and in a department that has close links with Downs' section. It seemed a long shot not to be missed.'

'It—it could have been a coincidence,' Aldona inserted, not very pleased with his Sherlock Holmes bent that hadn't allowed him to let up.

'It could have been,' he agreed smoothly, 'but it wasn't, was it? At this time of year your father must have been working closely with Downs, must have spoken with him on more than one occasion. It seemed quite within the bounds of possibility that if they'd been working late getting the books ready for inspection then Downs could well have given your father a lift home, could easily have met you.' He broke off to give her a shrewd look. 'That's how it happened, isn't it? You met Downs at your father's house, didn't you?'

All her senses were working overtime. She was battling with all she knew not to let Zeb see that with his talk of getting the books ready, Downs working closely with her father, he was getting much too near for her liking to stumbling on the real truth. She knew if she allowed him to see she was terrified should he accidentally press a question remotely connected with those books, she would give away there was more to know lying just beneath the surface. There was only one way to keep his astute mind from picking up anything, and that way was to brazen it out. Striking an uncaring pose, she pushed her hands into the pockets of her jacket.

'Yes, I met him at my father's house,' she said loftily. 'Fortunate for me, wasn't it?'

'As I remember it, you weren't so keen to stay with him when I showed an interest.'

'You'd already told me you weren't a poor man,' she said, watching his lips tighten at her blatant manner. 'And anyway,' she added, playing it for all she was worth, 'you've just said yourself—he's fat.'

Zeb's lip curled with derision that that hadn't bothered her before he had come on the scene, and that derisive look upset her too, so that she plunged in and asked if he had already learnt she was Roland Mayhew's daughter before she got there.

'No,' he told her. 'I discovered on going through your father's personal file, reading his references, that he's considered a wizard with figures and finance. It gave me a good excuse to call on him if I wanted some urgent advice on a certain financial matter. He's known for his integrity,' he added, implying that the advice he wanted was on a confidential matter, and giving her a look that said the same couldn't be said for his daughter's integrity. 'Business out of the way, I asked after his family, then as he was telling me he had recently married, his first wife having died nineteen years ago when his daughter was five, I heard the front door open. Before I could ask after said daughter you came bursting in looking so horrified to see me there that I straightaway knew not only had I found the girl I'd been looking for, but that you were scared witless in case your father learned you weren't the sweet and good little girl he'd always thought you to be.'

'My father has heart trouble,' she told him again.

'I did know before you mentioned it. There's a medical report in his file.'

'Then you must see that you can't—can't at some later date use me in—in your mother's divorce, it would kill him!'

Zeb didn't repeat that she should have thought of that before, but just stood and looked at her, his chin showing agression that she was telling him what he could and could not do.

'Please,' she begged, her pride in ashes, 'please forget I was ever in Malta.'

She saw his eyes go over her pale face, saw them rest on her mouth, before travelling down over her unbuttoned jacket that revealed her white shirt, her breasts thrusting forward, and down over the long length of her thighs and legs, and she thought she would go demented as she guessed what was coming.

'I wonder if it'll be worth it,' he said slowly, then as she ran a despairing hand through her long dark tresses, he said quietly, 'Come here.'

Her feet felt like great lumps of lead, but she knew he wouldn't move towards her. The ball was in her court. The next move was hers.

Slowly she moved forward, her eyes wavering when he didn't look away but watched her approach with a coolness she would have given anything to have possessed just a fraction of just then. She stopped walking when she was just a pace away from him, half expecting him to say, 'Now kiss me,' but he didn't.

Then very deliberately he reached for her, and unhurriedly, as though knowing she wouldn't, couldn't back away, he pulled her the rest of the way until their two bodies were touching.

'If my memory serves me right, the taste of your lips is an experience a man might lose his head over,' he said softly. And while her eyes flew wide to hear him say such a thing, his head came forward and down and he was again tasting that experience.

At first she struggled, but it was an instinctive move of self-preservation. And Zeb lifted his head and waited until she had got herself under control, still holding her, but by no means forcing her. Then his head came down again, and this time she didn't struggle. Not even when, her lips firmly closed, before that tingle he had disturbed in her before made itself felt, did she struggle. Then that thrill of his touch was working inside her again and though she might hate this weakness in her he had found, her lips parted and she could do nothing to hold back her response.

She felt his hands beneath her jacket, felt her spine melting at his touch. Her arms came up and around him when he pressed his body closer and she moved in, because she wanted to be nearer still. She faltered when his hand came to cup her breast, and pulled her mouth away from his, gasping, her eyes opening, her startled look surprising him into taking his hand away.

'Oh, Zeb!' she cried, and it seemed to come from the very heart of her, her bewilderment at all that had happened, all that was happening, and most of all bewilderment that he could make her want his hand back on her breast again, yet if he placed it there, not knowing how she could save herself from wanting more.

'I want you,' he muttered, looking down at her, his voice coming thickly from his throat as his hands went to her hips and he pulled the lower half of her up against him. A groan escaped him as if the contact with her was overcoming his clear thought processes. 'Help me, Aldona, I want you!'

She sensed some sort of agony going on inside him, and because the feel of him against her was causing her sensations she had never felt before, and had no guideline to know what to do about them, she stayed quiet.

Her arms were still about him when he groaned, 'I've got to have you—but not like this. Not by blackmailing you in payment for keeping your father from knowing about you.'

The sensitivity in him was showing itself again, but at the mention of her father, some semblance of sense rushed in. Here she was in the arms of a man who had the power to destroy him, and heaven help her, something untried, unfelt before, was keeping her there. She moved her head as though hoping that would clear it and found Zeb had released her hips and now had one hand to the back of her head and was burying his head in her cloud of dark hair, pressing her head into his shoulder.

And then he was pushing her away, looking every bit as though he hated himself as much as he hated her, and all she stood for. She knew then that he had mastered his desire for her, and felt cold without his arms around her. She had the clear impression he would leave her now.

'Are you—are you going to—go through with ...'

'With keeping your name ready for the time my mother decides enough is enough?' he interrupted her grittily, and when she didn't answer, 'No,' he snapped explosively, adding, 'I don't want your father's demise on my conscience.'

Aldona wished she could believe that, wished she could believe that when she hadn't contacted Lionel Downs and he had adjusted the books to show her father's guilt, he wouldn't be just as guilty of killing him when he prosecuted him, as he would be if he had her named as co-respondent.

'But you want me?' she asked, not stopping to wonder where on earth the idea that had just popped into her head had come from, but knowing she would have to come out with it and quickly. For by the look of him, once he left, it was going to be the last she ever saw of him.

Zeb looked her over, and she thought she saw a flicker of desire in his eyes, though the rest of his face was expressionless. 'You know that much,' he said.

But she knew much more than that. A few minutes ago, had it not been for that fine sensitivity, she just knew he would have let his masculine urges rule him. But the thought that it would be blackmail to get her co-operation had hit him hard, and though he badly wanted her, those finer feelings in him had come out on top.

'You could ...' The thought of what she was about to say was sticking as if glued to her throat. Her hands were moist, and for all it was a cold night her shirt was clinging to her back with perspiration. She forced herself to go on, seeing he was waiting stern-faced for her to continue. 'You could still—h-have me if you would—pay,' she said, and felt the awful stillness of him as her words reached him.

'What did you say?'

She knew he had heard her the first time and felt a rush of hatred for him that he was going to make her repeat it before he told her his answer. That momentary hatred fired her courage.

'I said, if you pay me the three thousand we agreed on, I'd—I'd . . .' Courage ebbed at the furious look he flung at her.

Then in a stride he was up to her, his one hand cupping her chin in a grip that threatened to break her jaw. Then very slowly he ground out, 'You disgust me!' and pushed her away with such force she lost her balance and fell backwards on to the settee.

He didn't even look round to see where she landed, but as though if he stayed in the same room with her for another moment he wouldn't be responsible for what he did, he strode to the door.

The door was still reverberating from the crash with which he had slammed it behind him a minute later. But by that time Aldona was past caring. She was huddled over on the settee and crying as she had never cried before. She felt cheap, dirty—and was further away from saving her father than ever.

CHAPTER SEVEN

ALDONA awoke the next morning and dragged herself out of bed, fully aware that the night had done nothing to carry away the heaviness of her thoughts. But thoughts of Zeb, his disgust with her, had to be forced to the background. Her uppermost worry was that she could delay no longer than tonight in going to tell her father that at some time in the near future, maybe as early as tomorrow the matter he had thought was covered up had been revealed by the auditors.

She was working the later shift that week, and it was around mid-morning when she was in the kitchen, her mind not on what she was doing, she emptied a packet of tea into the teapot instead of the caddy, that Mrs Armstrong, who had happened to come in at that moment, asked:

'Are you all right, Aldona?'

'I'm fine.' Her response was automatic as she saw what she had done and set about rectifying it, expecting Mrs Armstrong to collect what she had come in for and leave.

But Mrs Armstrong didn't leave straight away. 'If you'd like a couple of days off to adjust,' she offered kindly. 'Wendy's back now and ...' Her voice tailed off as Aldona gave her a quick look, not understanding why Mrs Armstrong should think she needed to adjust. Then it came to her that she must have been going about with a very long face, and was giving the impression that she was upset because of her broken engagement.

'That won't be necessary, thank you all the same, Mrs Armstrong,' she said, and knowing she was letting her carry on with her belief that she was brokenhearted, for all it served as an excuse for the way she must have been since seeing Lionel Downs on Sunday, she added, 'I'd rather be at work.'

'As you wish,' said Mrs Armstrong, a bracing note in her voice before a glimmer of humour showed itself. 'But if it's your turn to make elevenses, could I have coffee?'

When she had gone Aldona tried to see the humour in what she had said. She wasn't the only one who pre- ferred coffee for their morning break, they all did. But she was hard put to it to summon up a smile.

After that she made a determined effort that no one else should see that while her body might be at her place of work, her mind was not. And when at three that afternoon she was called to the office to take a phone call, she was fairly confident that though she had a lot on her mind, from the cheery exterior she presented, no one else would know how inwardly churned over she was feeling.

As she heard Barbara's voice on the line, panic that Lionel Downs had not waited until midnight tonight as he said he would threatened to take over completely. Barbara had never telephoned her before. Had her father been brought home ill? Was he already in hospital? Was he . . .? She couldn't finish the sentence, but had to quickly sit down, only to hear Barbara saying quite brightly, which she wouldn't if he had suffered another heart attack:

'I hope I haven't called at an inconvenient time. But I judged you might be taking a breather just now.'

Vaguely Aldona was aware of assuring Barbara that she hadn't interrupted her during a minor crisis, and then her stepmother was telling her the reason for her call.

'Actually I'm calling to put you off coming to see us tonight. Liz Richards, a friend of mine, has just rung to ask if I can use two theatre tickets. It's a play I know Roland particularly wanted to see, but,' her voice became slightly hesitant, 'but if you . . .'

'Of course I don't mind,' Aldona said hastily, having made great strides recently in her friendship with Barbara and not wanting to go back to the awkward way they had been with each other, because there was a bond of affection growing between them.

'You don't have to limit your visits to once a week,' Barbara was saying, while Aldona was wondering what did she do now. 'And it doesn't have to be a set night, does it?' There was a pause, then Barbara was saying, 'I'd like you to feel you can drop in at any time.'

The warmth that had come to her at Barbara's keenness that she should feel part of the family faded once the phone was back on its rest. She couldn't tell her father tonight, that was for sure. Perhaps she was being cowardly, she admitted, in leaving it until the very last moment to tell him, but being used to getting up early and since she wasn't due to start work until nine-thirty tomorrow, she could call and see him first thing in the morning. That way he could enjoy the theatre, goodness knew when he would enjoy another play, and he could also have another night's rest without the stress and worry that would consume him if she went round later that night.

Because she knew all her reserves of strength might be called on after tomorrow, Aldona prepared a meal when she arrived at her flat that night. But when it came to eating it every mouthful tasted like chaff. Half of it went in the waste bin, and then because she knew she had to keep busy, she changed into working jeans and a casual top, did some washing and then spruced up her already tidy flat.

At ten past nine she had run out of chores. Reading was out of the question, as was writing letters or anything else she could think of to occupy herself with. Then salvation came with the sound of someone knocking at her door. Debbie from the flat below come up for a chat, she thought, ready to welcome her with open arms if she was the means of keeping her mind from going round and round in the same horrific circle.

But it wasn't Debbie who stood there as she flung back the door with a welcoming smile stamped on her features.

'Oh!' she exclaimed, surprise uppermost, as for all he was casually attired in grey trousers and a navy sweater,

Zeb Thackeray stood there, the briefcase he was holding
denoting he had either not long finished work, or that there
were important papers in his briefcase that he didn't care to
leave in his car.

Aldona could hear her heart pounding in her ears as
she looked at him. The disgust he had felt with her last
night was not in evidence, though she didn't doubt he still
felt the same about her. At a loss to know why he had
called, she just stood staring at him, her brain momentarily
numb as though hoping some bright remark would present
itself. Then as the only words that roared in her ears were
the remembered ones she had uttered when offering herself to him last night, a hot searing red coloured her face,
and she didn't have to say a word, for he observed her
heightened colour and spoke the first words to her since
that 'You disgust me'.

'You need to blush,' he said coldly. 'Though I would
have thought you would have left your blushes behind
after your first few clients.'

If he'd come here purely to insult her, then she could
well do without it. She refused to budge from her position
by the door. If he had anything to add to those three words
she had found so wounding last night, he could say them
from there. She didn't doubt they'd be short and to the
point.

'I'm well aware of what you think of my morals,' she
said, her colour dying, leaving her pale. 'And if you've
called to give me a lecture on what nice girls don't do,
then if you don't mind, I'll take it as read.'

'It's precisely because you do what "nice" girls don't
that I'm here,' he told her. Then sardonically, 'Do you
really want to discuss your fee out here on the landing? A
very *nice* girl let me in, but I'm sure she's still hanging
about to see whether she was right to do so.'

She had the door wide at this, 'Do you want to discuss your fee out here on the landing?' feeling sick and excited at the same time. Zeb closed the door after him and as an icy coldness settled over her, she found herself inviting him to sit down. He chose a chair opposite her, and she was glad to have the occasional table dividing them.

'You mentioned "fee",' she reminded him when long seconds stretched with him not saying anything, but just sitting there with a cold look on his face. She was sounding greedy, she knew, but she couldn't let that worry her. Couldn't let it worry her that if—and it was still a very big 'if' at the moment—but if he was prepared to hand over the money she had asked for, then she would not have to think at all of what came after, but could concentrate solely on what it would mean to her father, to his life or death, to keeping his embryo marriage as happy as it was at present.

'I see you're a girl who likes to get the most important matters out of the way first,' he remarked. How hard his eyes were when he looked at her like that!

'You were the first to mention it,' she said, not liking that he was putting her on the defensive, and going into the attack. 'Do I take it I no longer disgust you?'

'Oh, you disgust me all right,' he told her coolly. 'I disgust myself too,' he added. Then he told her flatly, which threatened to have the colour surging to her face again so that she was glad of the icy calm that had come to her, 'But I want your body.'

'And ... and you're prepared to pay?' she asked, clinging desperately to the calm she felt was doomed to desert her at any moment.

'I need to get you out of my system,' he told her bluntly, letting her know that once he had slaked his desire that would be the end of it for him. 'If the only way to do that is to part with three thousand, then yes, I'm prepared to pay.'

What she was supposed to say or do then Aldona didn't have a clue. 'I—er——' she began, her calm bolting as the full realisation of what she was doing hit her. Her mother would turn in her grave, her father would join her if he had an ear to this conversation. Then as it struck home that he would anyway if Lionel Downs didn't have his three thousand pounds in cash by midnight tonight, the word 'cash' leaping out from all others, she forced herself into the terrible part she was playing, and said, 'I'm sure you won't mind in the circumstances if I ask for the—the fee in—er—cash.'

Not taking his eyes from her, Zeb dipped his hand down to the side of his chair where he had placed his briefcase. Then still watching her, he found the handle and lifted it, opening the briefcase in one movement and turning to show her the contents.

Her eyes flew wide as she saw the neat bundles of currency there, her heart setting up a terrific hammering as she turned her startled eyes to his.

'Thought that would make your eyes light up,' he said cynically, placing the briefcase between them on the table. 'That's my part of the transaction completed. Now it's your turn.'

What was she supposed to do? Go across to him? Fling herself at him? She stayed where she was, a trembling taking hold of her that if he made a grab for her she was now his to do with as he wished

'W-would you like a coffee?' she asked, and knew that was the last thing he expected her to say as he gave her a quizzical look. 'I—er—was just on the point of making myself one when you called,' she lied.

'Far be it from me to deprive you of anything,' he said,

overcoming his surprise. 'In fact I think I'll join you.'

For a moment as she got to her feet and made for her tiny kitchen, Aldona thought he meant join her in the kitchen, and that wasn't what she wanted, because she needed some minutes alone to think. But Zeb made no move to follow her and she realised he had meant only that he would join her in having a cup of coffee.

She put the kettle to boil, took out the instant coffee and a couple of cups and saucers, checking her watch as she did so. It was now nine-thirty. Some time before midnight she had to make that call to Lionel Downs. A dreadful thought struck her that had her clutching to the table top. What if Zeb intended to stay all night? She swallowed hard, fighting for control. Aside from the shame of the other tenants in the house knowing she had had a man in her flat all night, though she herself had met a few strangers on her way out early in the mornings, no stranger had ever left her flat and met the milkman calling. Did Zeb intend to ... Did he mean to ...? Her mind didn't want to tackle it, but it had to be faced. Was he going to make love to her before he left? The kettle boiled, and she switched it off as she groped for some answers. For three thousand pounds he would consider he had brought himself a mistress for however long it took for his desire for her to wane. She mustn't think about that side of it, she mustn't. The important thing was to get down to that telephone in the hall and make contact with Lionel Downs.

She switched the kettle on again and set about making two cups of coffee, then took the tray into the other room, setting it down, loath to touch the briefcase as she pushed it away to make room for the tray on the table. Then with fingers that weren't quite steady, she handed Zeb his cup.

In a silence that stretched her nerves to the limit they drank their coffee. Then just as she had returned her cup to the tray, he asked, his voice conversational almost.

'You were engaged until recently, I believe?'

She was glad to hear him say something, feeling she couldn't have stood the heavy silence for very much longer, and talk about her engagement suited her better as a topic than anything else he might have chosen to talk about.

'Yes, that's right,' she answered.

'Who broke off the engagement? You, or,' as if he thought it more likely, 'him?'

It wasn't any of his business, but still thinking she was on nice safe ground, she decided to keep the conversational ball rolling.

'I did, actually.'

'Were you in love with him?'

With what he thought of her fixed in his mind it surprised her that he credited her with such a feeling. 'Yes,' she said, and flicked a glance at him to see he had an aggressive look about him, as if he didn't like to hear her confess that. Well, he wouldn't, would he? He wouldn't like to have his opinion of her misted by a suggestion that she wasn't as hard as he thought.

'So why give him his marching orders? Did your head rule your heart? Wasn't he able to give you *everything* you wanted?'

She had no idea why he was being so aggressive, though she thought it probably had something to do with the fact that the disgust he felt for himself and her had been buried beneath his need to possess her.

'I *was* in love with him,' she said, keeping her voice quiet and hoping it would tone down his aggression. She was fully aware that by his *everything*, he thought she and Guy had been lovers, but that Guy's pockets hadn't been up to her expensive tastes. 'I discovered it wasn't the genuine article after all.'

'How long ago was this?' he asked, some of his aggression fading. 'When did you come to the conclusion that you no longer loved him?' She knew full well when it had been. It had been the Tuesday before the Saturday she had flown to Malta. 'When exactly did you break off your engagement, Aldona?' he pressed when he could see she didn't want to answer. He was like a dog with a bone, she thought crossly. And because he looked set to sit there all night if she didn't tell him, she said, 'If you must know, it was three weeks ago tonight.'

Silence reigned for only a brief while as Zeb worked it out as she knew he would. Then, 'You really weren't in love with him, were you? Less that a week afterwards you were going off with Downs,' and harshly, 'What's the matter with you? Are you so man-mad you couldn't wait for someone nearer your own age?'

And she'd thought his aggression had faded! 'If you cast your mind back you'll remember he paid me two thousand pounds,' she said, his aggression firing her own.

'The two thousand you couldn't wait to spend on clothes,' he bit back.

Strangely his temper subsided then. She saw his glance go over her and it was as if he had just noticed she was dressed in jeans that had seen better days, and a top that could be purchased for next to nothing at any market. For a girl who thought that much of clothes, she knew as she saw him take in her attire that he couldn't be blamed for thinking she didn't care what she wore to lounge around in.

'Tell me,' he said, and his voice, though alert, almost silky in comparison with the way it had been, 'what clothes exactly did you buy with the money he gave you?'

She should have thought of something brighter to say she had spent the money on than clothes, she thought, but she had not expected to have to give him an inventory.

'Er——' she faltered, thinking that if she gave him a lofty 'this and that' it would hardly cover that amount of money. 'A fur coat,' she said, having no trouble remembering that was what the original two thousand had been spent on. Then as she saw from the look on his face that he might not be swallowing that, alarm struck that he had enough gall to go and check her wardrobe himself if the mood was on him. And further alarm that, dear heaven, she wanted to keep him away from her bedroom as long as possible. 'It's rather a lovely thing, actually,' she said. 'I'd show it to you, only my father has taken Barbara to the theatre tonight and I've lent it to her.'

Whether Zeb believed her or not was hard to tell, for his expression was suddenly inscrutable. Though why he shouldn't believe her was a mystery. As much a mystery to her as was the thought that kept popping into her head that he was neither making any move to leave nor, since as he had said he had completed his part of the transaction by passing the money over, was he making any move to get her into her other room.

A surreptitious glance at her watch showed it was half past ten. Where had that last hour gone? Her agitation to have him leave, to be able to get down to that phone, made itself felt.

'I expect you'll—er—want me to come over to your place,' she said, deciding since he was making no move she'd got to be brazen.

'Is that what you usually do?'

Already she was out of her depth and the conversation hadn't got started yet. 'Well, I expect your place is a bit more—er—comfortable than mine.' She thought it was rather clever to trot out the, 'I've only got a single bed,' that came to her on a flash of inspiration.

Zeb gave her a smiling look that was clearly suspect. 'You've never before made love in a single bed?' he queried.

'You're taller than average,' she said, hearing the girl that wasn't her talking, and feeling astounded that she could keep up with this verbal fencing.

The smile she had suspected of having a sting behind it showed itself for its true worth. 'We're not going to my flat,' he said.

'Are—are you intending staying—er—overnight?' She knew her voice had risen as the girl she really was took over.

'I'm sure I wouldn't be the first.'

The untruth of that remark hit her in more ways than one, and a fresh sort of panic came as a thought struck her she had been too busy thinking of other things to think about. Oh lord, what would he do when he found out he was the first? He'd know then she had been speaking the truth when she'd said she hadn't been to bed with his stepfather. But he was sure to question what she had been up to in letting him think she went to bed with all and sundry.

'I ... I ...' she began, and stopped. Her brain could only deal with one thing at a time. She had to get her thoughts in order of priority. 'I have to make a phone call,' she said, intending to add that it would only take two minutes then she would be back with him. But he didn't allow her to add anything.

'I'll come with you,' he said smoothly.

'There's no need. The phone's only on the ground floor.'

She stood up, only to find Zeb had risen too. 'You ran out on me once before,' he reminded her. 'I'm sure you won't mind if I cover my money with a little insurance.'

Blankly she stared at him, then catching on, 'I'll leave the money here,' she said quickly. 'Look, I'll leave my bag. I shall only need a few five pence pieces for the phone.'

Her agitation getting on top of her, she took her purse from her bag, straightening up to see a look on his face that told her she was wasting her time arguing. He had every intention of going to the phone with her whatever the argument she put up. Well, having got this far, having said she had a phone call to make, she definitely was going to do all she could to get her phone call made without Zeb having any idea who she was calling.

With the scrap of paper with the number she was to dial safely tucked away in her purse, she turned to leave her flat, the straightness of her back showing a mutinous line as Zeb accompanied her. Praying that Lionel Downs himself would answer the phone, that he would under- stand and be agreeable to the 'Oh hello, Jane, Aldona here. I couldn't make it tonight, can you come over to- morrow?' she had prepared, she took the scrap of paper from her purse and holding it closely to her so he shouldn't see, she dialled the number.

The last digit didn't complete its journey before the phone was taken out of her hand and violently slammed down. Then before she knew what was happening she was back in her flat, having been hauled there by a raging Zeb, who slammed the door shut with a force that left her in no doubt, should she have misread that raging look on his face, that he had followed every digit she had dialled and knew full well who she had been calling.

'Why?' he rapped. Just the one word, but they both knew what he was asking.

'I ...' she began helplessly, and swallowed hard when he gripped hold of her upper arms, looking ready to shake the living daylights out of her. He did shake her, just once, and if that was a foretaste of what was to come as her head rocked on her shoulders, she knew, since he wasn't going to ask again, that she'd better start talking.

'I w-wanted to tell him I had his money,' she said huskily, knowing his eyes were piercing into her, but too scared to meet them.

'You intend to pay him back his—outlay!' He shook her again, and she knew from that as much as from his tone that he didn't believe her.

'He's insisting that I do. I t-told you I'd seen him once since he came back. He called here asking for his money.'

She wasn't sure whether it was because what she had said tied in with what he knew of the man that Zeb now looked ready to believe her. But at any rate his stinging grip on her arms lessened, and then he let her go, watching as she rubbed the soreness on her arms and thrusting his hands into his pockets as though to save himself from the temptation of inflicting further hurt.

'And you intended to return his money?' he asked sceptically. Then, his eyes narrowing shrewdly, 'Why was it so important you tell him straight away you have the money? You haven't earned it yet.'

He could be really charming when he chose, she decided, but now wasn't the time to go into character analysis. He had a tough, hard look to him, a ruthless look she imagined he would use in the boardroom if the occasion demanded it. He would brook no opposition when he went after something he wanted, she could see that. And he was waiting, his temper on a short fuse, for her to tell him just why she had to ring Lionel Downs without delay.

'Why?' he snapped aggressively, his hands coming out of his pockets, nothing about him casual as he looked poised to grab hold of her again and force the words from her lips.

'H-he wanted to know by midnight tonight that I had the money,' she said hurriedly, taking a rapid pace backwards out of range as those hands came up as though to take hold of her.

'You were expecting me to call tonight?' he thundered, his temper suddenly exploding, and there was nowhere she could run to as his hands came towards her in a lightning movement and he was hauling her mercilessly up to him, the look in his face showing he didn't take kindly to being played for a sucker.

'No-no,' she said, absolutely terrified. He looked set to murder her, and as tall as he was she couldn't help feeling shattered that so much aggression could be housed in one frame. 'It wasn't like that,' she gabbled. 'He was insisting I paid him. Threatened to ...' Oh ..., that was wrong. He had her so frightened she hadn't a clue what she was saying. 'He wanted his money and I didn't ...' She stopped right there, had been going to say she didn't know where to turn to get the money. But already she had said too much, and defeated tears sprang to her eyes. If Sebastian Thackeray was hellbent on murdering her if she didn't tell him any more, then he would have to get on with it. To add anything to what she had said would have him knowing the lot.

A tear spilled over on to her cheek, and after so much storming violence in the air, a hushed sort of silence seemed to settle on the room. Her arms were suddenly free, and a strangely gentle hand was on her face, wiping the tear away.

'You said he was threatening you?' said Zeb, his voice quiet after the raging fury he had spilled over her. 'What hold has he over you, Aldona?'

Panic started up within her again, this time at how near to the truth he was getting. Had it been his intention to harm her before she knew that wasn't his intention now.

And with him not roaring at her, her brain, that had been a conglomeration of emotions rather than thought, was able to think with at least some hint of her natural intelligence.

'Is he blackmailing you?' Zeb asked, his voice still quiet, controlled.

'He said if—if I didn't return his money by tonight, then tomorrow morning he would—he would tell my father I'd been away with him. My father—he would have another heart attack,' she explained, her voice dying as the truth of that smote her again.

'So it is blackmail,' he said, his tone hardening.

'Please, Zeb,' she begged, finding the courage to look up into his face since it looked as though he believed her version of why Lionel Downs was blackmailing her, 'please let me make that phone call.'

'You intend to give in to his threats?'

'What else can I do?' Then remembering that row in Malta, she reminded him, 'You yourself had to back down at the threat of your mother being hurt.' She could see he didn't like to be reminded of the frustration he must have felt then. 'I love my father the same way.'

'I know you do,' he said shortly, causing her to feel a peculiar dart of joy from that brief but sincere statement, that in her love for her father, if nothing else about her, he had every trust.

'Then you'll let me make that phone call?' she asked, her heart lifting.

'We'll do more than that,' he said, going over to the table. 'We'll deliver it personally.'

'Oh, but——' she began to protest, her spirits dropping once more, then as she saw him taking out some of the bundles of notes from the briefcase, 'What are you doing?'

'The amount you owe him is two thousand, isn't it?'

'He wants th-three thousand.'

Had she imagined his expression had softened any?
It proved to be an illusion. For his face looked to be
carved out of granite as he bit out, 'Hush money?' Though
he did fling the notes he had taken out back into the briefcase before aggressively snapping it to. 'Get your coat,' he
commanded.

The panic that seemed to be as much a part of her these
days as breathing was with her as she did his bidding and
went into the bedroom for her jacket. In her old jeans and
top she wasn't dressed to go calling anywhere. But with
the recent trauma she had been through, that point seemed
incidental. And now that Zeb was being coldly horrible
again, she didn't relish any of his sarcasm if she closed
the bedroom door while she changed. As it was, she was
nearly going under with the thought that Lionel Downs
might let something slip about her father's weak moment.
She preferred to call it a weak moment because it still
didn't register that he was a thief.

Zeb picked up the briefcase as she joined him, but before he had gone more than two strides to the door, one
ghastly fact hit her, and her cry of, 'Oh!' had him halting
in his stride to look at her.

'Y-You told me your mother is still living with—him.'

'True,' he said tightly.

'Oh, Zeb—I can't meet her.' The very thought was
making her feel ill.'

'What's the trouble? Can't you face the blameless party
in all this—filth?'

He knew how to hurt. And Aldona wished at that
moment she could have told him how it really was. Told
him that the 'filth' he spoke of nauseated her so much that
she was sure she would have nightmares about it for years
afterwards.

'Don't bother,' he said harshly, seeing she was not deny-ing it. 'I wouldn't let her breathe the same polluted air as you. I'll go in and see Downs. You can wait in the car.' Panic again that Lionel Downs might let something slip. 'Or,' he added, seeing the whiteness of her face, 'don't you trust me to hand the money over?'

It didn't need thinking about. 'I trust you,' she said, and found herself blurting out. 'I never slept with him, Zeb, I swear it! He got drunk that first night and ...'

'We're wasting time,' he said, and could just as easily have said, 'You're wasting your breath,' she thought, as they left her flat and went to his car.

CHAPTER EIGHT

ALDONA'S thoughts were too jumbled as Zeb drove in the direction of his mother's home for her to take any notice of where they were going. But it was after about half an hour of driving with nothing more than a morose silence coming from him that he slowed the car and swung it round a semi-circle of a drive and stopped in front of a large stone-built house.

Aldona sat where she was as he leaned over to lift the briefcase from where he had tossed it on the back seat, then opened his door. She knew if she moved one muscle as though to go with him she would earn herself a few short, sharp, unpleasant remarks. He needn't worry, she had no intention of going in with him. But she was sud-denly feeling stifled and when the door closed after him she did move, but only to open the window on her side of the car and feel the cool air fan her face. It was air she badly needed when before Zeb had gone more than a few strides the front door opened and the figure of a woman came down the steps to meet him. The woman was of medium height, but as Aldona caught a flash of silvery hair, she knew with certainty that this was his mother.

'Zeb!' the woman exclaimed. 'I thought it was you. I was just going to bed when I saw your headlights flash across the window. How nice to see you,' she said, adding humorously, 'even if you do time your calls to see your mother when most decent people are going to bed.'

Quiet as a mouse, Aldona stayed where she was. Zeb's mother sounded so nice, and with all she had on her conscience, she just didn't want to meet her.

'Only a brief visit, I'm afraid,' she heard him say, a softness in his tone that was at odds with the way he spoke to her. 'I'm away from the office tomorrow,' she saw him raise the briefcase aloft, 'and I want Lionel to take some papers in for me.' His voice still with that soft note there, had an edge creeping in that Aldona was aware of, though she wondered if his mother was, as he asked, 'He is in, I suppose?'

There was a pause before Mrs Downs replied, and when she did her voice had a resigned air to it. 'He's been in the study all evening.'

Aldona gathered there was very little point of communication between husband and wife, and she wouldn't mind betting whether he was working or not, that he had been freely imbibing. Then all thought ceased as Zeb put his hand beneath his mother's elbow to escort her back into the house, and she heard her say:

'Aren't you going to introduce your friend, Zeb?'

How she thought she'd got away without being spotted by Mrs Downs, Aldona couldn't think. Because standing there a few yards away from the car, for all she hadn't peered through the glass at her, Mrs Downs couldn't avoid seeing her shadowy figure sitting there.

'Of course,' she heard Zeb say, 'though Aldona won't thank me for it. She was in the middle of her chores when I dragged her out for a drive.'

She had about five seconds to calm herself before her door was opened and a firm hand on her arm was propelling her out on to the gravel. Five seconds in which the fleeting thought had struck her that he had somehow discerned that her embarrassment at meeting his mother wouldn't be helped at all that she was dressed as though on her way to a tramps' ball. And five seconds were nowhere near enough for her to gather any sort of composure around her, though she thought her, 'How do you do,' was fairly audible as Mrs Downs shook her hand and invited her to come inside.

'You can't sit out here while Zeb conducts his business. I don't know what you're thinking of, Zeb!'

To think not at all would have been Aldona's wish as the three of them went into the house, where Zeb left them and she went with Mrs Downs into a most delightful sitting room with plain walls and chintzy furniture, the sort of room she could never imagine Lionel Downs contributing to.

She sat down as she was invited to, but refused a drink of any sort. To accept further the hospitality this kind woman was offering was something she just could not do. Mrs Downs' hair was white, not silvery as she had first thought, and her face, fairly free from wrinkles, told her that for all her white hair she was no more than about fifty-five. She was doing her best to draw Aldona out too, to make her feel comfortable, asking about her work and showing such a real interest when she told her she worked looking after toddlers, that had she not been feeling so guilty Aldona felt she would have really opened up.

'Have you known Zeb long?' Mrs Downs went on to ask, when the subject of her job had come to a dead end.

'Not too long,' she answered, unable to stop from wondering what Mrs Downs made of a relationship that hadn't been going for 'too long', but could have been said to have progressed by leaps and bounds since her son felt he could call and 'drag her out' regardless of how she was looking. 'We met at a party,' she felt impelled to lie, because her previous answer had sounded so stilted she felt more guilty than ever that Mrs Downs was having to do her best with such an awkward guest.

'Did you?' she questioned, her face showing mild surprise. She smiled then, the same grey eyes as Zeb's twinkling. 'Forgive me, Aldona, but from what I know of Zeb, and from what he chooses to tell me, he does all he can to get out of going to parties.'

'Oh,' said Aldona, feeling awkward again and searching round for something to add that wouldn't be another blunder.

'Still, I expect he's glad he made an exception to that rule,' Mrs Downs added, and Aldona knew from that that her hostess meant he had been glad because he had discovered her there. Then before she could say more, Aldona heard the rattle of the door behind her, and hoping it was Zeb, but fearful to turn round and check in case he had Lionel Downs with him, she stared down at her lap.

'Ready?' asked Zeb.

Awash with relief as she looked up and saw he had come in by himself, Aldona got to her feet, heard Zeb refusing his mother's offer to stay for a coffee at least, heard him say he would be in touch, and add a final sentence which Mrs Downs didn't look beneath the surface of, but which set up a hammering in her own heart, 'I must get this young lady packed off to bed.'

The car was pulling off the drive and was on the road before the hammering in her heart slowed to a trot. Then Zeb was taking something from his pocket as he waited for an oncoming car to pass, and as he accelerated he dropped a piece of paper into her lap.

'What's this?' she asked, holding on to the paper that would have fluttered to the floor.

'A receipt,' she was told shortly. 'Proof that I've handed the money over to Downs.'

'A receipt?' she echoed, having not doubted he would do as he said.

'Any debt you owed him is now cleared—— Your outstanding debt now belongs to me,' he said significantly.

Aldona remained quiet. What was there to say in answer to that? Part of her anxieties began to lift as the car sped through streets she began to recognise as familiar. And as the thought grew, and with it an ease from some of her worries, that at last her father was safe, she missed entirely that Zeb had cut off from the road that should take them to her flat, and it was some ten minutes later, with only one worry, enormous as it was, in front of her now, that she looked out to observe they were heading towards the motorway.

'This isn't ...' she began, then, her seemingly constant companion fear back with her again, 'Where are you going? You've missed the turn,' she told him, hoping the simplest of explanations would prove to be the real reason for them being miles away from her flat. 'My flat doesn't lie this way,' she added, trying to stay calm when Zeb didn't answer straight away.

She was sure it wasn't because he had picked up that note of fear in her voice that he eventually deigned to say something, but what he said did nothing at all to quiet her fear.

'I thought we'd go to my place,' he told her.

Wishing she'd never closed the window, feeling hot inside, Aldona forced herself to think of practicalities. Having no idea how far out his flat lay, but sure now it was the motorway they were heading for, she wondered how she was going to get to work on time tomorrow if he didn't feel inclined to take her.

'You'll bring me back in the morning?' she asked weakly, wilting under the pressure of the thought that the night had to be got through first.

'You offered Downs two weeks for less than I paid,' he said succinctly.

But succinct or not, she couldn't believe the implication behind his words. 'You mean I'm to stay with you—for more than just—one night?'

'For three thousand I intend to have more than one night with you, fair Aldona,' he said casually. 'And since you've been known to duck out on a deal before, I'm ensuring that you won't easily do so again.'

Feeling weak at the knees that he had given no indication how long she would be away, the question left her hurriedly, 'But what about my job? I have to be at ...'

'You work as *well*?' he interrupted. 'Your moonlighting business must be falling off!'

The weakness left her at his belittling tone. Anger flared and she just didn't know how she prevented herself from hitting him. For too long she had been acting the role of someone totally at odds with the person she knew herself to be, and it was touch and go whether the person she really was would stay down. Her control never greater than at that moment, she held hard on to the almost insurmountable urge to attack Zeb, concentrating with all she knew on checking the need for physical violence that had never before been a part of her nature.

From then on she said not one word, and after what seemed like hours of driving, though probably wasn't because he must have his flat somewhere near London, the warmth of the car got to her. She tried to keep awake, began to mentally recite poetry in an effort to keep sleep away, but, tired from lack of sleep the previous night, emotionally exhausted, she finally found rest as her eyelids closed.

It was irritating to have a hand shaking her awake. She didn't want to come alive to a situation her subconscious was telling her this time there would be no escaping from.

'You'll sleep much better in a bed,' a hard voice roused her. And piercing through the mists of sleep came shrieking a shaft of knowledge that she wasn't tucked up in her flat and alone. She was still in the car and Sebastian Thackeray was still her companion.

She opened her eyes, was aware of a throbbing pain in her head and saw light streaming from a cottage, its front door open indicating that Zeb had gone and opened up before returning for her. Cottage! Her sleep-filled brain sprang into action.

'I thought we were going to your flat,' she said, making no attempt to get out of the car. 'Where are we?'

'Breconshire,' he told her briefly, then equally briefly, 'Move.'

The cottage had a charm all its own—not fussy, but with an air of warmth about the place. It was late September now and they were going through a cold patch. If Zeb lived and worked in London as Aldona was sure he did, then shouldn't the cottage feel cold? He could have been here last weekend, not alone either if she was any judge, but surely any heating in the place last week would long since have evaporated.

'Do you use this place often?' The question left her before she could stop it.

'As often as I can,' he said behind her, urging her along the small hall and into the sitting room. 'And in answer to the other question I saw in your eyes, I haven't brought anyone else here. I have a perfectly adequate flat in London for the purposes you're thinking of. This is where I come when I want a spot of peace and quiet.'

She paused at the door of the sitting room and wondering at his reference to the times he wanted peace and quiet, her glance flew to his. She realised then that for a man who ruled the massive company he did, then there must be times when he needed to take time off to 'get away from it all', a place he needed where no one could easily reach him. Was this his sanctuary?

'No one's likely to find you here,' she said, following her train of thought.

'We don't want to be disturbed, do we?' he replied mockingly, an answer she could well do without.

With him so close behind, she was forced, if she didn't want his body to touch hers, to move forward into the sitting room. The air there too was warm, but the first thing to catch her notice was her suitcase she had last seen above the wardrobe in his room in Malta.

'My case!' she exclaimed, having thought she had seen the last of it. It had never entered her head that he would bother to bring it back with his own luggage.

'You won't be needing very many clothes while you're here,' he taunted. 'What you have in there should be more than adequate.'

'You've looked through my things!' she exclaimed, a hint of anger in her voice that he could do so, tinged with embarrassment that he should sort through her white cotton briefs and bra's.

'You'd just tried to rook me of three thousand pounds. I didn't see any good reason not to check for some hint of your identity.' He wasn't taunting now, and she could tell his own anger was only just beneath the surface. Then he added, his anger going from him as curiosity took its place, 'For the *femme fatale* you're made out to be, I saw little evidence of anything in there likely to turn a man on.'

Aldona didn't want him curious about her. 'Not all men go in for women in black lace,' she retorted, indignation that he had gone through her things to the fore.

'I'll agree. I can get equally excited at seeing a female covered in a white cotton shift.'

Indignation fled, as scarlet colour flooded her face, the remembrance roaring in of the way Zeb had moved the white cotton of her nightdress from her shoulder, the way his hand had caressed her breast.

'Blushes?' he queried, his voice showing a slight puzzlement. 'What sort of thoughts are raging through your sweet mind, Aldona?'

'I'm not blushing,' she lied. 'It's—it's hot in here.' He wasn't fooled, she knew that, but he didn't follow it up.

'It is warm,' he agreed. 'I left a message for the woman in the village who looks after the place for me asking her to come and put the heating on.'

'It wasn't a split-second decision to bring me here, then? You had it planned?'

Zeb didn't answer. He didn't need to, she saw that. 'Are you hungry? Do you want anything to drink?' he asked abruptly—so abruptly that Aldona fired back the answer without thought.

'No—to both questions.'

'In that case, we'll go to bed.'

Sickness grabbed at her, and what he had just said was

doing nothing to relieve the pain in her head that was now aching severely.

'H-have you got any aspirin?' she asked, and felt violent pugilistic tendencies towards him when he asked sarcastically:

'Migraine?'

'No,' she said, knowing that only the truth was going to be believed.

'Then,' he said, 'perhaps we can find a better cure than aspirin.' And by then he had taken her into his arms and Aldona had not only to contend with a stomach that was madly churning, and with a pounding head that was stabbing at her, but also with a heart that had begun banging out a fast-beating rhythm in opposition.

She was close enough to Zeb to see the tiny lines around his eyes, but as she just stared up at him, her face pale, he in turn was looking into her eyes, seeing for himself the strain there, observing for himself the way she involuntarily winced when he turned her face up to the electric light so he could see her more clearly. And then any other leading remark he might have made was never spoken.

'Are you sure it isn't migraine?' he asked quietly.

'Positive,' she said, and had no idea why she being so honest.

Though as the word registered with him she felt that her honesty had earned her one good mark at any rate, for his arms dropped away, and indicating the nearest chair, he instructed, 'Sit there for a while.' Then without waiting to see whether she had complied, he picked up her suitcase and left the room.

It was about ten minutes later when he returned, she thought. Ten minutes in which she had tried to keep her mind a blank. And then he was there handing her a glass of soluble aspirin, waiting patiently while she drank it, then taking the glass from her and placing it down on a table, he said, 'Come on,' and a guiding but firm hand was on her arm and he was forcing her to go into the hall and up the stairs with him.

He escorted her into what she thought must be the main bedroom, and when her hurried heartbeats topped by her headache and the feeling in her stomach caused her to be able to do nothing but stand there, her eyes glued to the double bed, he studied her still form and asked:

'Do you want any help getting into bed?'

'No.' The choked word came quickly as she recalled that other time he had stripped her naked before popping her between the sheets.

'In that case, I'll leave you to it—Goodnight.'

'Goodnight?' The exclamation left her as quickly as the word 'No' had done. 'Wh-where are you going to sleep?'

'In view of your indisposition, I think you'd better sleep on your own, don't you?' Not quite believing him, Aldona just stood and stared, and he came over to her to stand looking down at her. 'I've made the bed up in the spare room.' He then leaned down and placed a kiss on her slightly parted lips, then stood back, his eyes lingering on her. 'If I don't go now, I shan't go at all,' he muttered. Then, showing he still had some self-control, he strode from the room.

Dawn had broken when Aldona awakened. She knew after that first second of opening her eyes where she was, and lay for another few seconds for everything that had happened in this room last night before Zeb had left her to flash through her mind. Then she took another few seconds to marvel at the sensitivity in him that had made him, for all he had made no bones about wanting her, leave her when he had known about her pounding head. Then as she remembered also that he had once said that love in the morning got the day off to a good start, she had the covers off the bed and was on her feet, only then aware that the severe pain in her head of last night had gone.

Tension, she thought, as she extracted underwear, trousers and a shirt from her case, prior to tiptoeing to the bathroom and hurriedly washing and dressing. Was it any wonder she'd had a headache? she thought as silently, her feet making no sound on the thick brown carpet that covered the staircase, she went downstairs.

It was marvellous to feel tension-free, for a little while anyway. Zeb was still in bed and she hoped exhausted from his drive last night, likely to stay in bed for a few more hours yet. She went into the kitchen and made herself a cup of coffee, noticing as she took milk from the fridge that it appeared well stocked. And because she didn't want any other thoughts to intrude on this, her own few hours of peace and quiet, she deliberately turned her mind away from encroaching thoughts of how long Zeb intended they should stay here.

She took her coffee into the sitting room and from the window there gazed at the beauty of the view. She had never been to Breconshire before—wasn't it called Powys now? She had heard of the Brecon Beacons and of the Black Mountains of Breconshire and Monmouthshire, and was about to delve into the recesses of her mind to try and remember what else she knew about this Welsh county when a movement behind her had her turning round to see she had company.

Confusion hit her to see Zeb, a towelling robe about him, his legs bare and the opening at the top of his care-lessly shrugged-into robe showing the hair that grew on his chest, and she bent her head to take a sip from her coffee as she recalled that he had told her he slept without anything on. She couldn't even make a pretence of a cool 'Good morning' as she registered that he hadn't a stitch of clothing on beneath that robe. Then she found he wasn't expecting any greeting, as, her eyes averted, she heard him say mockingly:

'I took a look in your room. Couldn't you sleep?'

He moved then and came to stand close to her. If he had awakened in an amorous mood, goodness knew what she was going to do, for placed as she was by the window there was no way of escape. And as he came up to her, close enough for her to smell the earthy smell of his all male body heat, she knew he had placed himself to counter any move she made to sidestep him should he reach for her.

'I was looking forward to your welcoming arms,' he tormented, when not a sound had she uttered. 'It was—disappointing to find your bed empty.'

She didn't think she was going to be able to control her blushes if he went on like this for very much longer, and sought around for something to change the subject.

'Are you ready for breakfast?' she asked, pointedly ignoring his attempts to get her to rise.

'I had thought of having it in bed,' he told her suavely.

'I-I noticed there's bacon and eggs in the fridge,' she said, determined to stay on her own track, and knowing full well he had been baiting her when he gave an amused laugh and told her he was going to shower and would join her in ten minutes.

When Zeb joined her at the breakfast table, his hair a shade darker still damp from his shower, his mood had changed. No longer was he hell-bent on baiting her, in fact it seemed all he could do to talk to her, apart from a brief acknowledgement as she placed a plate of bacon and eggs before him.

Not that she wanted him to talk to her, she told herself, resenting him as much as she resented the feeling of being peeved that he could tuck into the breakfast she had cooked him as though she wasn't there.

When she heard the sound of someone opening the front door with a latchkey her eyes flew to his. 'Mrs Field,' he told her, and, his breakfast finished, went into the hall to come back with a small wiry-looking, overall-clad woman in tow. Aldona guessed this was the lady from the village who looked after him. His introduction was brief, and he added:

'I'm going for a walk.' Then as if that sounded too abrupt, though Aldona thought it was more out of courtesy to Mrs Field, who would wonder if they had had a row, than for any desire for her company that he added, 'Would you like to come, Aldona?'

She knew very well he wanted to be on his own, and that suited her too. 'I don't think so, thanks,' she said, her voice light for Mrs Field's benefit. She didn't have time to add anything else, because Zeb didn't wait to hear any more.

'I'll see to the kitchen, Mrs Field,' she offered, when Mrs Field began clearing the table. And when it looked as though she would protest, 'I don't feel like going out and it will give me something to do.'

'If you're sure,' said Mrs Field doubtfully, then when she could see the offer was sincerely meant, she smiled and confessed, 'I'm in a bit of a hurry today, I'll admit. I have another job in the village I usually go to on Thursdays, but I have to go to a funeral tomorrow, so if I can get done I thought I'd put Mrs Simmonds right this afternoon.'

Instantly Aldona offered her condolences, only to be told that it wasn't a close relative but a friend of her husband's they hadn't seen for years. 'We're only going out of respect,' Mrs Field confided. 'It'll be an early start for us tomorrow, though,' she added, explaining that the funeral was to be in Aberystwyth, and showed, for all her respect for the departed, that the friend of her husband's passing would be more of a day out for her as she seldom went anywhere.

Aldona got busy in the kitchen while Mrs Field went to 'do' upstairs. A 'niceness' in the way she had been brought up had her hoping Mrs Field would check the spare room and see, if Zeb had made his bed—she had been in too much of a hurry to get downstairs to make her own —that by the belongings he must have there, they had not shared the same bedroom.

She was busy making a casserole for lunch when Mrs Field reappeared and she found herself liking the woman very much when she stated, 'Mr Thackeray didn't say he was bringing a guest with him. I would have made up the spare bed had I known.'

So she had popped in there with her duster. 'It only took a minute to make,' Aldona smiled.

Mrs Field had been gone an hour when Zeb put in an appearance. 'Something smells good,' he commented from the doorway. Whatever had been bugging him at breakfast had been walked off, she thought.

'You've walked up an appetite?' she queried, seeing he looked in a good humour, her own good temper having been restored in the everyday actions of her labour.

'Is lunch ready now?' he asked, and she found herself laughing as she replied:

'It's only half past twelve.'

Really, she thought, as he helped her with the lunch washing up later, when he wasn't putting himself out to be horrible to her, Zeb was quite nice. Not one sour note had been sounded in the last two hours, and as he had

conversed with her over their meal with none of his remarks having the slightest suggestion in them that bed was
in his mind, Aldona began to feel more and more relaxed,
and couldn't help that the girl she really was came through.

'Like to take a walk through the village?' he suggested,
once the washing up was over.

'Love to,' she complied, feeling the need for exercise.
'I'll just pop up and get my jacket.'

There were signs on their walk that summer was over.
When the last horse-chestnut fell from that tree, Aldona
was thinking as they passed a magnificent horse-chestnut
tree, then its leaves would turn yellow. Zeb had shortened
his stride to match hers and she pulled her thoughts up
short as the thought came how she would love to be here
to see that gorgeous tree bedecked with yellow.

The cottage was some way away from the village, but
at last they came to a small cluster of cottages, then a
couple of shops, and when they reached the post office,
Zeb told her that Mrs Field lived in the house next to the
post office and since she was in there daily, it was to the
post office he rang to leave a message whenever he was
coming down. Once through the village, he thought to
ask if she was tired.

'Not a bit,' she said, thinking he was ready to carry on
for several more miles yet. 'I like walking, and there are
some beautiful trees around here.'

'You like trees?' he asked, and she smiled at him.

'Nuts about them,' she said, and knew he had observed
the way she had gazed in appreciation of the horse-chestnut
when he laughed at her unintended pun.

She was finding it amazing as they trudged along that
she could be so at one with him. It was as though he too
had forgotten everything that had led up to them both
being there. And Aldona found she was bitterly regretting

that she had come to know him the way she had. She felt
a pain that was almost physical at the thought that there
was so much that was ugly and sullied to mar any hope of
a lasting friendship between them. Lasting friendship! she
caught herself thinking. Then—oh no! But before she
could fully recognise what had happened to her, Zeb was
reminding her that she had referred to having a job last
night, and was asking what work she did. And she knew,
since he seldom said anything for nothing, that she had
to leave all other thoughts and feelings and concentrate
to the full on her answers.

'I work with children,' she told him, thinking it fairly
safe ground to tell him that, and that since she had told
his mother about her work he would know all about it if
her name came up when he got back anyway. From there
he drew her out and she went on to relate more or less
what she had told his mother, and when questioned further,
told him the part of London she was working in.

'You work with deprived children?' he questioned, nothing in his tone to tell her what he thought of her revela-
tions so far.

'The only thing they're deprived off is the attention of
their parents, or in some cases, parent, during the day,'
she said, never having thought of herself deprived in
having only one parent, and then unthinkingly, 'We try to
make up for the parental love they miss during the daytime.'

They walked in silence for perhaps about a minute.
Aldona had caught Zeb looking at her when she had
finished speaking as though he had picked up her unspoken
admission that she found it very easy to love the youngsters
in her charge and to give them the love that was absent
from their parents during the daytime. He had made no
comment, but seemed to be deep in thought.

'This job you do—does it pay well?' he asked suddenly.

Aldona felt a prickle of warning at his question, but the words had left her before she had time to heed it. 'Washers,' she said cheerfully, 'but I love it,' and knew she should have taken note of that warning when, in direct contrast to what they had been talking about, he challenged:

'What were you doing going away with Downs, Aldona?' and when she stood stock still and stared, he said, 'It's become obvious to me that your aversion to him is as great as my own. Just why did you go with him?'

Too late she saw she had been too free with her tongue. Zeb had lulled her into a false sense of security. Quite openly she had revealed herself as a girl who loved children, a girl who worked at a job that paid next to nothing. A girl who was the complete opposite to the girl who looked to have her eye on the man with the fattest wallet, the girl who would do anything for money. And from the quiet way he had asked his question, she just knew that Sebastian Thackeray of Sebastian Thackeray Limited was in charge of Zeb, and Sebastian Thackeray was a man who would demand nothing but the truth.

CHAPTER NINE

Now wishing she had kept up her guard, Aldona sought for some way to answer, her mind going through a rapid process of elimination. Lionel Downs had his money now and would not, she thought, bother her again. He had other fish to fry, he had said, so having found someone more willing to share his bed, she felt safe in assuming that his lust for her had abated. That being so, she could breathe easy that he wouldn't be putting his cunning to work on the company's books. But at all costs she had to prevent the head of that company from knowing what had gone on.

Zeb had halted with her, and when she risked a look at him, she could see a determination about him not to walk another step until she had answered his question. Bluff, she thought, was the only way out.

'You know full well why I went away with him,' she said at last.

'Ah yes,' he said, 'your urgent need of a fur coat. You wanted that coat badly, didn't you, Aldona?'

Some inner sense was picking up that for some reason he wasn't believing her. 'Yes, I did,' she agreed, the toe of her shoe scuffing over the grass as she stressed, 'I wanted that coat more than anything.'

'You wanted it so badly that you were prepared to spend fourteen nights in bed with a man you can't stand?' he challenged. 'Do you know, Aldona,' he remarked mildly— too mildly, she was wary of him now and didn't trust that casual tone, 'it strikes me as more than a shade odd that for a girl who's so obsessed with the idea of possessing a fur she doesn't care to whom she sells herself, has the said fur in her possession for less than a month, and then—when one could be forgiven for thinking she couldn't bear to let it out of her sight— she's lending it to her stepmother.'

'It's—it's not odd at all. I . . .'

'Isn't the truth of the matter that you haven't an avaricious bone in your body?' He ignored her attempt to interrupt as if she hadn't spoken. 'Isn't the truth of the matter more likely that with your job paying—washers, I think you said—you got yourself badly into debt? So badly into debt that you didn't know what to do about it?' Aldona stared at him, amazed by the conclusions he had drawn, but he seemed not to notice she was gaping. 'You could have gone to your father for help, I suppose,' he continued, 'but even if you could bring yourself to share your worry with him—and I've seen for myself that you're prepared to do anything rather than cause him worry—your pride wouldn't want him confiding with his new wife the fix you'd got yourself into, would it?'

'I've never been in debt in my life,' she flared hotly, as the pride he had spoken of roared to the fore. That was until he gave her a doubting look that caused the colour to rush to her face, and she could have died with shame that she was in debt to him for three thousand pounds and had as yet made no attempt to clear the debt.

'You're wrong,' she said stoutly, and having forcefully denied being in debt, was compelled to go on. 'Completely wrong. I wanted that fur more than anything, but —but Barbara had greatly admired it in my father's presence, and ... and because when they first married I wasn't too friendly with her, I wanted to show him that if I'd given him the impression that I resented her then he had nothing to worry about because I'd grown to like her very much indeed, to the extent of lending her my new acquisition. You've seen for yourself,' she reminded him for good measure, 'that I'd do anything rather than be the cause of worry to him.'

She saw the casual air had gone from him. He was now giving her close inspection, his face hard, and she thought him well on to half way believing everything she had told him.

'Where did he think you got the money to pay for it?' His words were clipped, as he asked the quick-thinking question that nearly tripped her up.

'He wouldn't know its value,' she said. Then, finding that when her back was to the wall her powers of invention were sometimes exceptionally brilliant, 'I told him I'd bought it second hand with my savings.'

Having sounded convincing, even to herself, when Zeb just continued to look at her with a hardness coming to his eyes that was frightening to see, she just knew she couldn't take any more.

'I'm going back to the cottage,' she said, instinct telling her he wouldn't be accompanying her.

'Do that,' he said tersely, and swung away from her, his long strides taking him rapidly from her side.

Aldoña set off back to the cottage, her mind dissecting every step of their walk, including the time they had come to a halt when Zeb had begun to question her and she had resorted to lying her head off. And in taking apart every word, every action, every emotion, by the time she arrived at the cottage it was all she could do not to sit down and howl her eyes out. For with all the mixture of words, emotions and soul-searching, only one very clear and irrefutable fact emerged. She had somehow, along the way, fallen in love with Sebastian Thackeray.

That there wasn't any sense to it, that he had been horrible to her more times than he had been nice, made no difference at all to the fact. For the times he had been horrible to her fell into obscurity, and only the times he had shown another side to him were with her. Times like the way he had chatted to her about some of Malta's history. The time he had looked after her when she had migraine. The way he had stifled his desire to take her that night when he saw she wasn't completely rid of her bad head. And the same last night, when that inner sensitivity had overridden his desire and he had dosed her with aspirin instead. And today, barely an hour ago, with everything she had ever told him all to the contrary—though she'd slipped up there in being too open about her job—but then he had looked ready to believe she was not as black as she had painted herself, had been ready to find excuses for her taking Lionel Downs' money. Why he had done so she couldn't fathom, but she had more than enough to occupy her thoughts without trying to delve into what went on inside his head.

It had gone eight when he came in and Aldona felt tension take hold of her as soon as she heard him at the door. Be natural, you must act naturally, she told herself over and over, but as she looked at him intending only to flick him a glance and away again, she just couldn't tear her eyes from him. She loved him! He looked cold and aloof, hard and as though he hated her, and yet she still loved him. Her feelings for Guy had never been like this. She dragged her eyes from him.

'Dinner's ready,' she said, having needed to keep busy in his absence. 'Do you want to eat now?'

'Might as well.'

Perhaps it was just as well that Zeb appeared to have no inclination to talk to her, she thought, as the meal she had prepared was consumed. This love she had for him was too newly discovered and she wasn't familiar enough with it to know any of the pitfalls one should look for if one didn't want the recipient of that love to be aware of it.

Tonight he didn't offer his assistance with the washing up as he had at lunch time, but went without a word into the other room. Wanting to see him, but afraid of his company, Aldona stayed in the kitchen for an age, growing more and more nervous as the minute hand on the kitchen clock turned round reducing the length of time before she would have to go upstairs.

Useless to hope Zeb had gone off the idea of wanting her, and yet he seemed in no hurry to chase her upstairs. She thought she heard a movement in the sitting room that shared a wall with the kitchen, and felt again her old enemy panic. She'd better join him. She could just imagine Zeb's aggressiveness if he had to come and haul her out of the kitchen, and though she was inwardly quaking at the idea of sharing his bed with him, had hurriedly buried the remembrance of the excitement of his kisses, she didn't want that aggression to be there the first time he made love to her.

He was sitting on the settee when she went in. 'Come in,' he invited, lifting his head from the technical-looking magazine he had been reading.

She closed the door behind her, her sights on the chair furthest away from him. He still had that 'no quarter given' look on his face and she wished she had a magazine she could read too so she wouldn't have to look at him.

About to walk in front of him, she felt a tingle of shock shoot through her as her wrist was taken in his grasp and seemingly without too much effort, she was pulled until she was taken off balance and had no choice but to sit on the settee beside him.

'Not feeling unfriendly, are you?' he mocked.

'Not at all,' she said, her heart thundering.

'Good,' he said, and moved up closer, his arm coming about her shoulders.

Aldona stared straight ahead wondering if Zeb could hear the thunder of her heart as it thumped against her ribs. Then she felt a shock of alarm that told her if he couldn't hear it, then he couldn't avoid feeling the riot that was going on inside her, for his hand slipped from her shoulder and was on her rib cage, his thumb a fraction from her breast.

'Not scared, are you?' asked that mocking voice. Then all mockery was gone briefly as he asked sharply, 'You *are* experienced in—these matters, aren't you?'

'Of course,' she replied, too bewildered by the suddenness of finding herself with his arm around her, the lead up to the reason why he had brought her here too much in the forefront of her mind to have her taking advantage of the chance to tell him that she wasn't.

Zeb accepted what she said without question. But as that thumb beneath her breast began a wayward investigation to the rise above, she was on her feet without being aware she had moved, or that her ejection from her seat had been so rapid it had caught Zeb by surprise and he had let her go.

'I—I think I'll go to b-bed,' she found herself uttering, and could have groaned at her stupidity.

'What a good idea!' The mockery was back, and on his face a look of the very devil. Aldona was out of the room before he added anything to that.

How long she dithered about before she finally took her dressing gown and nightdress into the bathroom and washed and got ready for bed, she couldn't have said. But no amount of pacing up and down and maidenly hand-wringing would alter the fact that she was about to meet her Waterloo. Though whether she would have made the transition from day wear to sleep attire was a debatable point, had not the thought come to her that Zeb had undressed her once, and she didn't doubt he would again if need be. And that if this was the way it had to be then she just couldn't bear to be put into bed again with no garment covering her.

It seemed to her strained nerves to be another hour before she heard footsteps on the stairs, and it was her cue to get into bed and quickly. She didn't want Zeb taking her robe from her, or anything else he thought unnecessary when he came into the room.

But he didn't come straightaway into the room and when she heard the plumbing go into action, intimating that he was taking a shower, she was struck again by the thought that he wasn't in any rush to claim her. And then the bedroom door opened and he stood there, dressed as she had seen him in the sitting room that morning, the towelling robe showing his bare legs and chest.

The bedclothes were pulled up to her chin, and he came round to her side of the bed, his eyes not missing a thing of what he could see of her.

'Your face is flushed,' he remarked, 'your eyes wide and threatening to pop. Do I go and fetch the aspirin?'

Sarcasm she could do without. 'I haven't a headache, if that's what you mean,' she said with a coolness that belied her looks.

She thought some other comment might be coming her way, but found she was mistaken as Zeb gave her one last hard look, then went to the light switch by the door and plunged the room into darkness. Then he was getting into bed beside her.

Whether the fact that she was trembling got through to him, she had no idea, but from that hard look he had given her, she had thought his lovemaking would be as harsh as his expression. But there was no sign of harshness or roughness about him as he silently reached for her, pulling her towards him. And his kiss, when it came, was gentle, his hands not urgent at her waist, and a wave of love floating on a tide of gratitude that afterwards she would have this tender memory of him washed over her, and tears came to her eyes.

And yet, loving him as she did, the very way he was being with her making her want to respond, something inside was making her hold back. What that something was she didn't know, only recognising it had little to do with her strict upbringing; it was something within herself that just wouldn't let go.

She was unaware that she was crying until Zeb moved his hand from her waist to stroke the side of her face, and then a change came over him. She felt a stillness in him as though her tears had shocked him, and aggression was there in that voice in the darkness.

'Why the tears?' he asked, his voice sounding thick and rough.

'I don't know,' she answered honestly, and sensing that any second she would be hearing sarcasm, that this memory wouldn't be the tender memory she wanted, she pleaded quickly, 'Don't m-make it horrible for me. Please, Zeb—please stay gentle.'

'Make it horrible for you?'

She heard from his voice that he didn't understand her plea. And then as though her nearness to him in her thin cotton covering was wiping out all but the urgency that was coming to him, he smoothed away her tears, then kissed her at first gently, then with a growing passion that she couldn't deny had her wanting to respond to him.

Her arms went round his neck as his chest lay over hers, and naturally in shy response her lips parted beneath his. And as his hands caressed, causing her thinking to be temporarily suspended so that she could only feel the same urgent need growing within her for him that she knew he had for her, she was overcome with shyness when wanting to touch him in return her fingers came into contact with his naked chest and she pulled back, finding the freedom she wanted to allow herself too much when she barely knew him.

It was a one-sided lovemaking. And though her body wanted to respond, shyness she had never before been aware of had her in its grip, so that when Zeb's mouth left hers and he said aggressively, 'Stop holding back, Aldona,' all she could say was a husky repetition of what she had said before:

'Please—be gentle with me.'

She knew she was being pathetic, knew Zeb thought so too as his full aggressiveness came to life.

'Why the hell should I?' he demanded.

She wanted to scream at him to go back to being tender with her the way he had been, but she knew that tenderness had gone from him and would stay away unless she gave him some good reason.

'B-because I'm—not experienced,' she whispered, and felt again a stillness in him, a shocked stillness, before, terrifyingly, she found her confession not believed.

'Like hell you're not!' he grated.

Then as though some demon was in possession of him, he tore her nightdress from her, and was assaulting her senses violently with a kiss that left her breathless and hands that roamed her body as though they had every right to do so. Not seeing any shyness in her, he had no concession to make as his lips and hands found her breasts.

Her senses whirling, Aldona's hands came into contact with his body, and helplessly she lay there, wanting to touch him but frightened of the emotions he was arousing in her. She wanted to do more than just hold his shoulders, thought he was expecting more, but was finding her inexperience at war with her need.

Then the fingers that had been caressing the crown of her breast ceased caressing, his lips left hers, and she sensed a calm before the storm. She knew her senses had not played her false, when briefly he moved away from her to switch on the side lamp, then was back again and she was able to see into his face and knew the storm was about to break. He looked violently angry.

A cry was wrenched from him. 'You haven't a clue what to do, have you? You can't even fake it, you're so terrified.' He shook his head as though to clear it from all thoughts of what he now knew to be true. 'You haven't been with a man before, have you?' he grated.

'No,' she said on a thread of sound, and wished she had lied when he looked more furious than ever on hearing her confirmation.

He muttered again. 'To think for the sake of a *bloody fur coat* you were ready to sell your virginity to that ...' His voice exploded on an awful name he didn't apologise for, and with one movement he had swept her up in his arms, taking her with him as he moved to put out the light.

It was at that moment Aldona knew that this was no trial run. Zeb might violently object to her selling her virginity to Lionel Downs, but she knew then that by tomorrow morning, although to a younger man, her virginity would have been purchased—and claimed.

His mouth was over hers, feverishly ravishing, as though some devil was riding him at what she had done. And it was then when his hands moved over her body, the tempo of his lovemaking taking on an intense urgency, that it came to her, as she tried to keep his questing hands from her, just why she hadn't been able to give him the response he wanted.

Alarm grew, a desperate anxiety about her as she fought him. The realisation that had come to her, making her twist and turn to get away from him.

'No!' she screamed, but to no avail as Zeb pinioned her beneath him so she should not escape. 'No, I can't,' she cried, and knew she would fight him to the end.

'You've left it too late to find out you can't,' he said, then told her ruthlessly, 'We're past the stage when there's any decision to make—you're going to be mine, my lovely.'

'No—No!' she screamed, trying to scratch at him. 'I can't!'

Had it been in mutual love she would have rushed to

meet him. But his talk of the fur coat, his reminder that she was going to be his because he had bought and paid for the privilege, was something nothing in this world would have her living with. It made her no better than a lady of the oldest profession, and she just couldn't take that it should be so with the man she loved.

She was crying in earnest as she broke away from him, becoming hysterical that he seemed so set on taking her that he couldn't hear her cries of 'No!'

'Don't!' she cried, her voice sounding strangely high-pitched in her ears. She hit out at him wildly. 'I can't bear it!' she screamed, her voice rising higher. 'Not with you, not with you. No—no—not with you!'

She came out of her hysteria to find the light had been switched on, that both she and Zeb were breathing hoarsely, and that he had been shaking her. '... All right,' he was saying, 'It's all right. I've got your message loud and clear. You can't bear me to touch you, can you?'

Only vaguely aware of what had gone on since Zeb had put the light on for the second time, Aldona stared at him, his bare chest rising and falling, his face cold. If he still felt desire for her it wasn't showing in that cold face. Then she became aware that she was sitting in a position similar to him in the middle of the big bed. Instinctively her hands went to hide her breasts from his view as she saw his gaze flick over them. Then he was retrieving her dressing gown from where it had fallen from the bed to the floor, instructing her curtly to cover herself up, and was shrugging into his own robe.

'Dry your eyes,' he ordered, then his voice coldly cruel. 'If you go on like this every time some man tries to score then it's no wonder you're still a virgin!'

Then while she could only sit there, her eyes large and moist, he gave her one last look as though to satisfy himself that her hysteria was a thing of the past, and left her. She heard the thud of the spare room door being closed, then all was silent.

Gradually, as the next hours passed, a calmness came to her that had her chaotic brain patterns sorting themselves out. She had gone from high-pitched emotion to a sort of numbed coldness. And as the darkness of the sky gave way to a deeper blue, and then dark grey and dawn began to break, Aldona knew that for the second time in her life she was going to run out on Zeb Thackeray.

That he had left her as soon as she recovered from her wild state, she put down to a temporary respite. He had given her no indication of how long they were to stay at the cottage, but for all the fineness of his feelings she couldn't forget he was an eye for an eye man. She just couldn't stay merely for the same scene to be enacted to-morrow night or perhaps sooner.

When she silently left the cottage, she had left nothing behind, not even a note. She had stripped the bed, neatly folded the sheets and blankets, and knew when Zeb came looking for her the finality of that would tell him she hadn't merely gone for a walk. Those folded sheets and blankets would tell him she did not intend to spend an-other night in that bed; that she wasn't coming back.

Her feet followed the route to the village they had taken yesterday, and she checked a sob as a knife blade turned in her that on this part of their walk yesterday there had been a feeling of a growing friendship in the air. She mustn't think about any of those good moments with Zeb, she thought, common sense urging her against useless dream-ing. Somehow she had to get back to London, and the quicker the better. Should Zeb wake early and come look-ing for her then he would be furious and would, she knew, take no notice if hysteria threatened another time.

Perhaps someone in the village ran a taxi service, she thought hopefully as the first cottages came into view, looking at every window for a placard advertising such as she went on. Perhaps someone left the village early to go to work in the nearest town, she mused, not seeing any notice advertising a taxi for hire, and thinking somebody must be going into town. She'd make for the main road, it would be easier to get a lift once she was there if she hadn't got a lift before.

Her feeling of hope grew when she saw a shining Morris Minor 1000, parked by the post office, and a man coming out of the house next door, and her feet sprouted wings lest he should get in and drive away before she reached him. A woman came out of the house whom she recognised as Mrs Field, and her memory awakened to remember Mrs Field saying yesterday she and her husband were going to a funeral in Aberystwyth this morning. Had there been any hint in that remembrance that Mrs Field or her husband were deeply upset, Aldona would have given a thought to intruding on their mourning. But with the re-mark Mrs Field had made about it being more of a day out for her, when she reached them and Mrs Field had recognised her, she was able to put her request without her conscience pricking her.

'I was hoping to catch you before you left,' she said, smiling brightly, and hoping Mrs Field didn't think she had a cheek. 'Mr Thackeray will be busy with some paper work today, so I thought I'd go back to London. Do you think I could beg a lift to the railway station?'

'Why, of course you can,' said Mrs Field, having brought up three daughters, all safely married now, thank goodness, but having been jolted into the 1980s by their modern ways, and immune now to any surprises from their age group. 'That's all right, isn't it, Jim?'

Jim had rosy cheeks and the twinklingest blue eyes Aldona had ever seen, and not even his dark suit complete with black tie could take the merry look from his face, which she guessed would look full of humour even in his most solemn moments.

'Anything to oblige a lady in distress,' he said cheerfully, as he pushed the bucket seat forward so she could sit in the back. He gave her a solemnly cheerful look as he handed her case to her, and she knew then he had seen through her excuse, had guessed she was making a bolt for it, but was too much of a gentleman to enquire into what he considered her private business.

He hardly said a word after that, though Mrs Field kept up a constant chatter mainly about her daughters and her two grandchildren. Mr Field got out of the car at the station and Aldona got out his side to save disturbing Mrs Field.

'Have a good journey,' said Mrs Field.

'Thank you,' said Aldona, and because she couldn't very well wish Mrs Field to have a nice time in the circumstances, she offered another, 'Thank you,' and a big, 'Thank you,' to Mr Field as he gave her her case before getting back into the car and driving away.

A feeling of numbness was with her on her journey, that stayed with her for the rest of that day. It was still with her when she went to bed that night. At work the next day she went and found Mrs Armstrong to apologise for taking time off without ringing to stay she wouldn't be in.

'I would have appreciated you letting me know,' said Mrs Armstrong, letting her off lightly, 'but when you didn't come in I took it you were taking my advice and having a few days off.' She looked at the pale-faced girl, saw that her couple of days didn't seem to have done her a lot of good, and then a screaming match broke out within hearing distance, followed by a bloodcurdling yell, and she smiled at Aldona and said, 'I'm glad you're back. I think your presence is required!'

For the next couple of days Aldona lived in dread of a knock sounding on her door. Zeb might be back in London by now. She had thought he would lose no time in coming to say his piece. But as evening followed evening, and there was no sign of him, she began to realise he would not be calling.

As the days dragged painfully by, she was able to reason more clearly that there had been no reason for her to bolt the way she had done. She could only vaguely recall what had happened in her moments of hysteria, but had sufficient recollection to know that with that area of sensitivity she had witnessed in him, she must have banished completely any idea he had once had that he desired her. And even though he had plainly told her that no one defrauded him and got away with it, she knew she wouldn't be seeing him again. He must have decided enough was enough, she thought, and though three thousand pounds represented a small fortune to her, the amount would be minimal to him. And after all, what man would want to pursue a girl who had carried on the way she had done?

It was almost two weeks after her crack-of-dawn departure from the cottage and she had been home from work some ten minutes when at half past four her doorbell rang. She went down the stairs to answer it, and since it was Tuesday and she would be seeing her father later that night, she was both pleased and surprised to see him.

'Dad!' she exclaimed, pulling the door wider and closing it after he had stepped into the hall. Then as the thought came that at this time of day he should be at his office and could have telephoned her if he wanted to put off her visit tonight, a niggle of fear began to worry her. Knowing he wouldn't tell her any of the reason for his visit until they were in the privacy of her flat, she led the way, waiting only until the door was closed before she asked:

'What's wrong?' Something was wrong, she knew it. She hadn't seen that stern, authoritarian look about him since her last gigantic misdemeanour as a child. 'Has something happened?' she asked, fear gripping at her.

'You could say that,' he said, and as they both sat down, he went on, 'I had a row with Lionel Downs about an hour ago.' Was Lionel Downs threatening him again? 'One thing led to another,' he added before she could think further, 'and then he started getting personal—so personal I went for him. Only someone coming in and interrupting stopped me from giving him a bloody nose.'

'Oh, Dad, your heart!' Aldona gasped worriedly, only to be told shortly, more careless of his heart than his daughter:

'Damn my heart! I could have killed him for the vile suggestions he made about you.' Oh no, she thought, but he was going on. 'He disappeared before I could have another go at him, but as I began to cool down, one of the things he said began to tie in with other things that have happened.' He broke off to give her a sternly parental look. 'So now, Aldona, I want to know where you went that Saturday you were supposed to be going to Hilary's. You told me you hadn't gone because they were short-handed at work. But according to Lionel Downs, on that Saturday you flew with him to Malta.'

Oh, heavens above! It was bad enough that her father had lost his self-control long enough to go to take a swing at Lionel Downs. But to have to confess that he had been speaking the truth to her parent who had guided her along so many right lines—had shown in so many ways that he loved her without having to endorse it by putting himself at risk by losing his temper with that awful man— had her not knowing what to do for the best.

'I'm waiting, Aldona,' he said heavily, when her answer wasn't forthcoming, then impatiently, 'My stars, is everything he told me true? Did you go away with him, pass yourself off as his wife?'

Unable to answer, she saw her very silence was condemning her. But whatever he thought of her, she just couldn't tell him why she had done what she had. Then he was asking her another question, and she hated Lionel Downs afresh that he had done everything he could to besmirch her character.

'Is it true what he told me?' he asked sternly. 'That you spent one night with him, then when Sebastian Thackeray turned up you made a play for him and spent the next night with him?'

'Sebastian Thackeray—Zeb,' Aldona whispered involuntarily, knowing she had done nothing to convince her father she was anything other than what Lionel Downs had said.

'His call to the house had nothing to do with business, had it?' he pressed, then went on when she still couldn't answer, 'Remembering his visit, it was the one thing that stood out above all others as tying in with what Downs had said. Sebastian Thackeray called at the house because you hadn't told him where you lived and he wanted to see you again, didn't he?'

'Yes,' she whispered, hoping with all her heart that he wasn't going to ask why the owner of Sebastian Thackeray Limited wanted to see her again. Then she found she had no need to worry about it, for her father had put his own construction on why he had wanted to see her again. And as a long-drawn-out sigh left him, she saw he looked defeated, and was out of her chair and going to him as he said, attaching no blame to her:

'Oh, where did I go wrong in bringing you up? You were such a sweet innocent child.'

'You didn't go wrong anywhere, Dad,' she said quickly, her arms going round his bent shoulders. 'You're the best father any girl could ask for,' she told him. But he didn't seem to hear her as he went on:

'Was I too stubborn in my decision not to let anyone else take care of you when your mother died? I can see now I was. I should have listened to those who said you needed a woman's hand to guide you.'

Aldona listened to her father flailing himself as he considered all the blame his, that he had let her down by not heeding what other people had said, and she just couldn't take it. Far better, she thought, for him to know the whole truth, to know that she knew about the money he had stolen, than to have him fretting and worrying for what might be weeks on end that he had somewhere along the road failed her as a father.

'Listen to me, Dad,' she said, slipping from the arm of the chair and kneeling on the floor beside him, 'I know I've been made to look blacker than black, and I can't deny that I did go to Malta with Lionel Downs. But I didn't go with him because there's some quirk in my character you haven't been able to iron out.' His head lifted, and she saw she had his attention. 'I went with him because he said if I did, then he would see to it that the two thousand pounds shortage in the company's books would be squared.'

She didn't know how much more plainly she could put it than that without being too blunt. But she was astonished when her father not only grasped her meaning but said:

'But why should that matter to you?' And while she

was reeling that he had no idea how much she loved him or realised the fears she had had for his heart had been with her every move she had made, he was adding, 'You'd broken off your engagement to Guy before Lionel Downs went to Malta. I know you had, because Downs came back and told me after he'd given you a lift home that night, and I felt as though a ton weight had been taken from me.'

Guy? she thought, growing confused. What had Guy got to do with anything? 'Dad——,' she began slowly, 'I think we're talking at cross purposes. I went away with Lionel Downs because he said he would give you a cheque for the money you'd—er—borrowed.'

'Borrowed!' Roland Mayhew exclaimed as though thunderstruck. 'I didn't borrow any money.' Then as what she had said penetrated. 'Child, I didn't take that money. It was your ex-fiancé, Guy, who stole it.'

CHAPTER TEN

'Guy!' Aldona exclaimed. 'But ...' It was no good, she just couldn't take it in. Then as she looked at her father in amazement, she saw such a look of fury come over him that she began to fear for him.

'The *bastard*!' he exclaimed, his face working with outrage. She had never heard him use such a word before, she knew as he followed through his conclusions that the word was aimed at Lionel Downs, but was more concerned then with calming him down.

'Don't get excited, Dad, please,' she begged, her hand gripping his tightly. 'Please!'

He looked down, saw in her face the anxiety for him she was experiencing. 'Don't worry—I'm all right,' he said, patting her hand. 'I took the precaution of taking an extra tablet after my row with Downs.' Then, his expression returning to being stern, he said, 'You'd better tell me everything from start to finish.'

Haltingly, her eyes watchful for the first sign of collapse, but knowing him well enough to know he wasn't joking when he said he wanted to know everything, Aldona gave him a toned-down version of what had led up to her going away with Lionel Downs. She had no intention of him knowing anything of the terror she had experienced at the hands of Lionel Downs. Of Zeb she said nothing. And when she had finished she saw that her father was manfully suppressing the glint of tears she saw in his eyes at what she had done for love of him.

'Oh, my baby!' he groaned, an endearment he hadn't used for her in years chokingly escaping him, so that there were tears in Aldona's eyes too. Then, pausing to clear his throat, he told her that Lionel Downs had never given him a cheque for two thousand pounds, there hadn't been any need to replace the money once he had told him that she had broken off her engagement, going on to tell her that it was he who had found the error in the books and at that stage, not thinking anyone had made off with the money, he had straightaway consulted with Lionel Downs, who had traced the fraud back to Guy Stinton. 'Guy was on holiday then,' he reminded her, and informing her of something she didn't know, 'He never came back.'

'He didn't . . .'

'No. He must have realised he hadn't been as clever as he thought he'd been. Anyway, to go back to what I was saying. When I realised it was my future son-in-law who was the culprit, I could think of nothing but that you were going to be hurt when it came to light. I had no idea if he'd been in trouble with the police before—he could well go to prison, I thought. So,' and here he looked a little shamefaced, 'I went against all my instincts that told me I didn't want such a man to marry my daughter, thinking that if you loved him with half as much of the feeling I have for Barbara, then you wouldn't care what he'd done. So I asked Downs, who'd been very friendly to me since the first time he came to the house—I see now it dates back to the night he first saw you—anyway, I asked him if he could see his way clear to allowing me to repay the money and not to say anything about it. He said he would come to the house that night to discuss it. Only we couldn't begin to discuss anything until Barbara had gone out. I didn't want her to worry about me worrying at that stage. And then you arrived while I was upstairs looking for ...'

'But where were *you* going to get the money from?' she asked, startled. 'I didn't think you had that sort of money. That's why this whole thing got started, because I thought you'd—borrowed that two thousand to pay for the fur coat I saw Barbara wearing.'

'Fur coat?' he repeated. Then, 'Oh, you mean Barbara's pride and joy. *I* didn't buy it for her, it was a legacy from her cousin who died.'

'Oh,' said Aldona. 'Oh, Dad, I've been such an idiot!'

'We've both acted unwisely,' he agreed, 'for all that both our motives were for the best.' Then, his face taking on a black expression, 'But what grieves me more than anything is that for my sake you've sold your innocence to a man like that.'

'I didn't,' she said promptly, then went slightly pink. 'I couldn't when it came to it, and ... and then Zeb ...' She broke off, the pink in her face changing to red as Zeb's name fell into the air, knowing her father would not allow her to be silent about him either.

'What about Zeb Thackeray?' he asked, just as she knew he would.

'He was—very kind to me in Malta,' she told him; it was unthinkable that she should blacken Zeb's name to anyone even her father. Well, he had been kind to her, hadn't he, he'd put her to bed when she'd had migraine. 'I ran away from him before anything happened,' she said, and heard her father's deep sigh of relief, before he asked the question she had been dreading.

'If Downs got you to go with him to Malta on the pretext of having given me a cheque for two thousand pounds, then I can't see him letting you go without a fight,' he said with sharp perception.

'Zeb paid him three thousand pounds,' she said quietly.

'*Three* thousand pounds!'

'Lionel Downs said he wanted his money back with interest.'

'The louse!' muttered Roland Mayhew with feeling. 'So that's why Thackeray came looking for you—because he'd parted with three thousand pounds and you'd run away?'

'Yes,' Aldona agreed, not wanting to tell him any more.

'You haven't—settled with him yet?' he asked severely.

'No,' she replied, knowing what he meant.

'Good,' he said, and there was a wealth of heartfelt relief in that one word. 'Then I shall go and see him—see he has his money back,' he added with a determination she knew.

'But, Dad ...'

'It's the only honest thing to do, Aldona, you must see that.'

'Oh, I do, I do. But—but where are you going to get the money from?'

'Not by fraud,' he told her, getting to his feet. Aldona stood up too, seeing pride in every inch of him. 'Hoping

to be able to persuade Downs when he called that night
to allow me to repay the money Guy Stinton had stolen,
I'd arranged in my lunch hour to cash an insurance. I was
upstairs looking for the policy when you arrived.'

'Insurance policy?' she gasped. 'I didn't know you had
any insurance.'

'I don't have to tell you everything,' he said, a suggestion
of teasing lightening what had been a painful half an hour
for them both.

'Chauvinist!' she replied in kind, but was serious when
he went on to tell her he had let his instructions to cash
the insurance policy stand when he had learned that the
money would not be required for its intended purpose, and
he now had four thousand and some odd pounds in the
bank that he and Barbara had been deciding what to do
with.

'But won't Barbara mind you ...'

'No, she won't. I told her everything after it had happened, and she was in full agreement with my action.'

'Oh Dad,' Aldona sighed helplessly. Then, seeing the
look of strain about him, seeing he had gone through
much too much already, and that word 'honesty' hitting
her squarely between the eyes, 'Will you let me pay the
money back to Zeb? I owe him that much honesty at least.'

'You owe him ...' He broke off, suddenly seeing more
in her face than she would have wanted, as her thoughts
winged to the man she loved above all else.

Aldona found her eyes were misty after her father had
gone. It wasn't surprising really, she thought, for he had
guessed she was in love with Zeb and in an emotion-filled
moment, probably seeing for himself how hopeless her
love was, he had put an arm around her and given her a
tight squeeze before saying, 'I'll see the money is in your
account in the morning.'

From the moment he had gone, right up to the moment the following day when she went to Mrs Armstrong and told her she had some urgent business to attend to and could she have a few hours off, Aldona had been fighting an inward battle with herself. On the face of it there was no earthly reason why she shouldn't just send Zeb a cheque with a brief note explaining that she was now in a position to repay him his money. There was no earthly reason for her to send him a note at all even, just a cheque would suffice. Zeb would see her signature above the printed name and would have no problem in assessing that somehow she had gathered the money together from somewhere.

But there was something in her, hitherto unknown, that prevented her from taking that course of action, and kick against that inner self as she might she just couldn't break away from what it was telling her. And it was telling her that she must go and see him personally, must face him when she returned his money. Even while thinking he wouldn't be very pleased to see her, she'd like to bet he had been furious when he had discovered she had run out on him yet again.

Mrs Armstrong's permission obtained, at eleven that morning, dressed in her newest suit donned with the idea of looking her best, Aldona set off. Not wanting to arrive more flustered than she already felt, she took a taxi to the offices of Sebastian Thackeray Limited. It was a large building and the chances of bumping into her father were remote, though he would know why she was there and would probably give her a smile of encouragement to warm her on her way if she did see him. If she happened to bump into Lionel Downs—well, she felt so angry about him, it would give her a chance to deliver a few well chosen words.

She saw neither of the two men, and on asking the

receptionist if she could see Mr Sebastian Thackeray, she was headed off so politely, it looked as though she wasn't going to see him either. But she had not spent a wakeful night in rehearsing ten different ways of what she was going to do if this eventually arose, having thought it more than likely that an appointment had to be made well in advance to see him. Her heart was already playing nonsense when she found from the receptionist that he was in the building—he could so easily have been out.

'I should have mentioned that I'm a personal friend,' she told the receptionist, trying to convey without actually saying it that she would be in trouble if she didn't direct her to him. The receptionist gave her a look as though to say she had heard that one before. 'Look,' said Aldona, going on to plan B, 'I have something of his he left at his mother's home. I was over there last night and she asked if I would return it to him in person. She . . .'

It worked like a charm. She didn't have to perjure herself any further. The receptionist's natural smile thawed the pleasantly set smile with which she dealt with difficult callers. 'I'm sorry,' she apologised, 'but with Mr Thackeray being in Sweden for the last two weeks he's extremely busy today and his secretary said he wasn't seeing anyone. However . . .'

Minutes later Aldona was ascending in the lift, the directions the receptionist had given her the only clear thing in her mind. Now that she was within an ace of reaching her goal, the part of her that was definitely coward was tempting her to turn back and send Zeb the cheque through the post after all. But she knew she wouldn't be turning back. Even if Zeb did take exception to her interrupting what must be a very busy day if he had two weeks' catching up to do, she was feeling starved for the sight of him, and had to see him just this once.

After today she would have no excuse to contact him.

The lift stopped and she stepped out. And then she had no need of the receptionist's directions, for there striding along the corridor away from her was a tall, dark-suited man whose straight back she would know anywhere. She started after him knowing he couldn't yet be aware of her, her heart in her mouth and none of what she had rehearsed to say to him being remembered.

Zeb stopped at a door down the end of the long corridor which she thought would be his, and then as he turned to go in, his eyes swung casually in her direction, and then, the door open, he froze.

Knowing herself recognised, she could do nothing but go forward. But as she neared him, saw the ice in his eyes, saw the whole unwelcoming look he had for her, she wished with all her heart that she had obeyed what her cowardly instincts had told her to do and pressed the lift button for it to return to the ground floor.

'I . . .' she began, drawing to a halt a few feet away from him, and was saved strangling her vocal cords by trying to utter anything else, when a woman she guessed was his secretary came to the door saying:

'Oh, Mr Thackeray, Reception have just rung to say there's a young lady on her way . . .' Her voice tailed off as she saw Aldona standing there.

'She's here,' said Zeb in a voice that would freeze boiling water. And it was then that Aldona knew that he hated her, and she wanted to die. 'Would you kindly tell Reception,' he added, still in that same awful voice, 'that when I say I don't want to see anyone, I mean exactly that.' He didn't give his secretary time to say she would, but closed the door, letting a thoroughly demoralised Aldona know that anything she had to say to him could be said out here in the corridor.

Never was she more glad to find she still had a spark of pride left. Feeling crippled that he could hate her so, indicate so clearly to his secretary that Aldona Mayhew was one person he wouldn't care if he never saw again, she opened her bag and took out the folded cheque she had made out ready.

'You're obviously very busy,' she said, marvelling that she could sound so cool. 'I won't take up any more of your time. I just wanted to give you this.'

Zeb didn't even bother to look to see what she had given him, but favoured her with one more freezing look, then opened the door in a dimissive gesture taking her at her word that she wasn't going to waste any more of his time.

Aldona didn't wait to hear the door close, but was off down the corridor that seemed to be a mile long before she reached the lift, hoping she could hold back the tears until she reached her flat, going back to the nursery never entering her head, as she pressed the lift call button.

Though she had not intended to look back the way she had come, the sound of speeding footsteps had her eyes flicking in that direction. Then before coherent thought could penetrate, a livid-looking Zeb was up to her, the freezing coldness of him gone. His look was so furious as dark grey eyes almost black blazed down at her that her heart started to race to twice its normal beat as fear took hold. Then as the lift arrived and its doors opened, as though not trusting himself to speak he grabbed hold of her arm and pushed her inside before viciously stabbing at the button and sending the lift on its way down.

Aldona still hadn't found her voice when she was hauled out of the lift and past a goggle-eyed receptionist. Almost running to keep up with the man who had not let go of her arm since he had grabbed hold of it, she was forced to go with him out of the building and round to a parking area, where she was pushed unceremoniously into his car. Then he was roaring away from the building.

'Wh-where are you taking me?' she ventured, having been kept quiet by the shock and speed of everything that had happened, and not a little afraid of the fury on his face, now thinking it about time she said something.

'Shut up,' was the terse reply. 'I'm concentrating on my driving.'

She fell quiet, seeing for herself that he was in such a rage that to distract his driving in any way by arguing who did he think he was to tell her to 'Shut up' might have them both mixed up in a tangle of crashed metal.

Her alarm growing that all his rage was directed at her, she hadn't noticed where they were going, and when Zeb stopped the car, came round to her door and yanked her out, she saw they had arrived at a very smart part of London which housed some very exclusive residences. Then before the thought could more than touch down that this was where he lived, he was propelling her through the front door of one of the buildings and at a rapid pace ushering her into a lift, keeping grim hold of her as he set the lift in motion. And then they were out of the lift and entering an apartment that had huge windows that looked out over London, had a couple of deeply seated comfortable-looking settees, other furniture that looked equally comfortable to live with, and a carpet so thick it was like walking on springy turf.

Only when the door was closed and Aldona was standing in the centre of the room did Zeb let go of her arm.

'Now,' he said, volcanic aggression in every line of him, 'Now, you can tell me what the hell you've been up to!'

'Up to?' she queried, his fury terrifying her for all she tried not to show it.

'Don't play dumb with me, I'm in no mood for it,' he rapped furiously, and took her by the shoulders to give her a none too gentle shake, before quickly letting go of her as though he thought by not doing so he would forget himself altogether and make a thorough job.

He gritted, 'if you've sold yourself to anybody else, I'll kill you!'

'Kill me?' Aldona whispered, seeing he looked ready to do it. Then, as the meaning of his words got through, she gasped, 'You mean the money?'

'Of course I mean the money. Who gave it to you? Where did you get it?'

'I . . .' she began, then backed away before she could tell him it was her father, because whatever was going through his mind had him advancing towards her as though he did mean to murder her. She bumped into a settee and hastily put herself behind it, her whole body perspiring as she saw there was no reasoning with this man. Her fear of him must have reached him, she thought, and took a calming breath as he didn't follow her but stood where he was, and said:

'I know it wasn't Downs, so who was it?'

'How do you know it wasn't him?' she asked, and didn't know why she did, because the sooner she told him who it was and took some heat out of this situation the better. Though why it should matter to him who . . .

'Because for the last couple of weeks he's had a detective on his tail, that's why,' he answered aggressively. 'And the lady he's been visiting hasn't been you.'

'You put a detective on him?' she asked, forgetting her fear in her surprise. Zeb already had evidence he could use if it was needed.

'Not me,' he snapped. 'I've been out of the country for a couple of weeks. My mother rang when I arrived home

last night and told me his going off to Malta was the last
straw, and she's had a detective on him since the time I
went away. A certain Rosie Blake will be named in an
undefended petition.'

'Rosie Blake!' Aldona exclaimed. Rosie must have decided in Malta that she'd had enough of Eddie; she must
be the other fish Lionel Downs said he had to fry.

'You know her?' Zeb questioned tightly, and seeing from
her expression that she did, said, 'Not that it matters.
Downs is out now. More to the point . . .'

'Downs is out?' she questioned hurriedly, seeing his
aggression was rising again, but remembering the row
she'd heard in Malta, and Zeb saying he would have him
out.

'I had the greatest pleasure in—terminating his employ-
ment this morning,' he said, and from the way he said it,
she had a very clear impression that Mr Lionel Downs
had felt Zeb's hand on his collar as he had left. Then the
aggression she had suspected returning came back in full
flood. '*Damn you, Aldona,*' he blasted her, 'where did you
get that money? Who was he?' And then the settee was
no obstacle, for he was round it, his hands biting into her
arms as he shook her. '*Who was he?*' he roared.

'M-my father,' she managed to choke out when the
shaking stopped and he stood and glared at her.

'Your father?' he echoed, staggered. Then, harshly,
'Are you telling me the truth?'

'Ring him up and ask him,' she challenged, gaining her
second wind. 'He wanted to come and see you himself,
but I—I said it was something I should do.'

'You mean you've told him everything?—About you
wanting the money for a fur coat? About you and Downs?'
There was scepticism in his voice, though he wasn't raging
any more, which gave her the courage to confess:

'There wasn't any fur coat—at least there was, but it was Barbara's, not mine.' Aware that she wasn't making very much sense, she made a concentrated attempt to answer his question. 'Yes, I told him everything.' She paused. 'Well, everything except you and me at the cottage.'

She saw his mouth tighten, a whiteness about it, as if he didn't want to be reminded what had gone on there. 'Hm, the cottage,' he said, his scepticism falling away, to be replaced by a hard look. 'That was where you discovered you loathed the very sight of me, wasn't it?'

'I didn't discover anything of the sort,' she said hotly, the words shooting from her too rapidly for her to take them back. 'I—I—don't—er—loathe you,' she tacked on lamely, and saw his eyes were suddenly looking far too alert to let her leave it there.

'You're trying to tell me you didn't have hysterics when you thought I was going to take you?' he rapped sharply, that alert look still there.

'I—it wasn't b-because I loathed you,' she mumbled, hoping her brain would soon wake up and help her out, because she knew she was in danger of doing herself no good.

The hands that had been gripping her arms tightly now had her in a numbing hold. 'It wasn't?' Zeb pressed, seeming determined to have her revealing every last emotion she had experienced at that time. 'Why then did you repeatedly scream, "Not with you, not with you"? I gained a very definite impression that anyone else could have taken your virginity, but not me, because almost too late you discovered you hated me.'

Again the words were too quick to leave her. She couldn't, she just couldn't allow him to go on thinking she hated him, 'I don't hate you,' she told him, and saw some of the hardness leave him, though why she couldn't imagine, other than no one liked to be hated, even Zeb.

'Do you know, Aldona,' he said slowly, consideringly, a deliberate look coming to him, 'I really think you should back that statement up.'

'You don't believe me?'

'Let's say I think we should try a little experiment.'

She stared at him, having no idea at first what form his experiment would take. Then as those hands moved from her arms and went round her, pulling her inexorably closer to his body, she knew even before he asked:

'Shall we see now if you're going to get hysterical?'

And before she could reply, as the full intent of his purpose hit her, his mouth came down over hers and he was kissing her as though he really meant it. She knew then he was going to make love to her up until the point where he thought she would begin to go hysterical, and that thought alone was enough to have her struggling to get away from him. For now that the money had been paid back, there was absolutely nothing in the way of her responding to the full to the thrill of him. For her own peace of mind afterwards, for the sake of having to live with herself knowing she had given herself to Zeb while knowing it meant nothing to him, she knew she would have to fight.

'No—don't!' she protested when he broke his kiss to look into her wide brown eyes.

She wasn't hysterical in her protest, and he could see that, she knew, for his head came down again, and once more he claimed her mouth, parting her lips with his, his hands doing a mind-blowing sortie at the back of her beneath her jacket. She felt an exquisite pleasure tingle through her as she felt his warm touch in rapturous movement on her skin. He was making her come alive with his caresses, and the fight she had been determined to put up barely got under way as it was vanquished into surrender.

She wanted more, much more, and her arms went up and around him, her thinking turned completely upside down, so that she now wanted this moment to remember.

'Shall we try the settee?' he murmured against her ear.

Incapable of speech, she could only nod. And in a whirl of heightened senses, wanting his arms back around her when he let her go briefly to shed his jacket and tie, she went with him, her skin flushed as he then removed her jacket, remarking softly, 'You're looking a shade warm, Aldona,' then his arms were around her again and he was pressing her back into the settee, his long length stretching out beside her.

'Oh, Zeb!' she sighed, after a brief moment of panic on finding him unbuttoning her shirt when she had instinctively pushed his hands away. 'I'm sorry—this is all new territory for me. I—I—— Be patient with me.'

For answer, he kissed her gently, then easing her bra straps to one side, he kissed her shoulders, his head homing down to the sweet swell of her breasts. She moaned in pleasure and he raised his head to look deeply into her eyes.

'No hysteria?' he asked, and she could feel the pounding of his heart beneath her hand.

She smiled at him, her face a warm pink. 'No hysteria,' she confirmed, and then because she couldn't help herself, 'Oh, Zeb, I want you so!'

'You think I don't want you?' he asked, and smiled, so that her heart turned a neat somersault.

'Kiss me,' she begged, and didn't have to ask twice.

But something seemed to be holding him back, for after a kiss that left them both breathless, he didn't take up the advantage that was all his, but looked into her eyes again and asked softly:

'Why hysterics that other time? Why run away from me?'

'I couldn't stay,' she said huskily, nothing else seeming

to matter then but that he should kiss her again and take
her with him into this new enchanting world. 'I couldn't
let you make love to me then.'

'Why, my darling?' he asked, so gently that even without
that gentleness, she was ready to flip at just the 'my
darling'.

'Because—because—oh, Zeb, I couldn't—not for money
—not with you.' She closed her eyes again, because she
knew with that explanation out of the way, he would kiss
her again. Expectantly she waited. Then she felt his arms
go from round her, heard him move, and her eyes flew
open to see that he was sitting up, clearly having no intention of kissing her again.

Oh dear, had she been too forward? The pink of her
cheeks turned to a fiery red of embarrassment. She had put
him off by being too eager, too—too—— Oh no ...! The
sort of man he was he would be turned off by a woman
throwing herself at him.

In a terrible turmoil to be dressed and gone, she righted
her bra straps, buttoned up her blouse and struggled off
the settee, snatching up her jacket as she went. Where
were her shoes?—she had no recollection of taking them
off.

'Where do you think you're going?'

She didn't answer, couldn't look at Zeb, so mortified
did she feel, but having found her shoes, she stepped into
them and went racing for the door.

Zeb was there before she reached it, holding her with
one hand while he used the other to tip up her face and
force her to look at him.

'It's not hysteria,' he said slowly, then gently as before,
'What is it?' he asked, giving her an encouragingly warm
smile that made her want to cry. 'Panic at finding yourself in a land you've never travelled before?'

'I—you——' she began helplessly, damning her inexperience, for all he was looking kindly at her. 'I turned you off, didn't I, by b-being too—willing?'

She wasn't sure what she expected him to say to that, but she certainly wasn't prepared for him to burst out laughing. As far as she was concerned, it was the final humiliation. Her hand arced through the air as her pride refused to take such a blow. But before her hand could connect, Zeb had caught it, caught her wrist and retained it.

'I'm sorry.' Immediately on seeing how his laughter had bruised her feelings, he apologised. 'I wasn't laughing because you were pushy or too willing. You're so innocent in these matters, Aldona, will you believe me when I tell you I found your response shy and beautiful?'

Unable to answer, or even look at him now, she lowered her eyes. Then she felt the lightest of kisses on the end of her nose as though he was totally unable to resist doing so, before he told her:

'In view of your innocence I should be ashamed for wanting to know you completely.' Her colour flared as she recognised what he meant by that. 'But I felt no shame or remorse,' he went on, 'because I felt it was what we both wanted.'

Hardly aware of moving, she found he was slowly steering her back to the settee. Once there, he sat her down and positioned himself next to her, a light arm around her shoulders.

'I wanted to make love to you,' he told her. 'I still do. But that damned money cropped up again.'

'The money?' she queried, not understanding. The money had been paid back now.

'I was so mad when I looked and saw you'd given me a cheque that I tore the damned thing up the second before

I chased after you,' he explained. Then, going on to tell her why he had stopped making love to her, 'After you said what you did I began to experience feelings of guilt I didn't want. How could I take what you were offering, knowing that as soon as you found out you had three thousand more in your bank account than you should have, what had happened between us would turn sour for you?'

Again she was witnessing that finer sensitivity in him. He had wanted her, he was plainly telling her that, but not enough to allow him to forget everything to the exclusion of his desire.

'Thank you for explaining that to me,' she said, feeling suddenly very flat.

She would have got up and gone then, only suddenly something seemed to have registered with him. Something he had missed, perhaps, that only now had struck him. Aldona wasn't sure, but was aware as that arm tightened about her, refusing to allow her to move, something had come to him, and it was shaking him rigid.

There was a tremendous stillness about him, his voice husky at first as though some deep emotion had him in its grip, as he said, his voice gaining strength:

'I think you have some explaining to do, don't you?'

'You mean about how I came to tell my father about ...'

'That too,' said Zeb, and his voice became urgent. 'But explain something you said a while ago. I overlooked it at the time, being too busy trying to stifle my need for you.'

Aldona tried to think what he was getting at, but nothing came to mind. 'I can't remember saying ...'

'You said,' he broke in as though impatient to get something settled, and unable to wait, 'that with the money in the way you couldn't let me make love to you. You said, and I quote, "I couldn't, not for money, not with you".'

The grip of his arm was like a vice now as he urged, 'Just

what does that "not with you" mean, Aldona?'

Aldona inwardly squirmed. He just had to know from that that there was something special about him for her. And for a man with such a quick-thinking brain, if she had told him outright, idiot, idiot that she was, she couldn't have told him more plainly that she was in love with him.

'Let me go,' she begged, and fearful he would want her to put it into words, 'You know anyway.' Her mind in torment, she tried to get away from him, tried to leap up and make a dash for the door. But Zeb's arm was firm about her. He had no intention of letting her go anywhere.

Then unbelievably he was saying, with a tenderness she had never heard, saying as though he had a fair idea of what she was going through, 'How can I let you go, my darling, when to say goodbye to you would be like parting with half of myself?'

Astounded, she twisted round so she could see his face —and there she saw something that positively shattered her. She already had evidence that Zeb desired her body, but in his face she saw an expression she didn't dare believe in. For he looked like a man ready to lie down and die for her.

'Y-you ...' she choked, and nothing else came from her locked throat.

'I,' he said, his eyes not missing a thing about her, 'love you to distraction, Aldona.'

'But,' she gasped, her mind a jangle of hope and disbelief, 'you can't!'

'I can and I do,' he said, looking deeply into her wide velvety brown eyes, and seeing there that she wanted to believe what he was telling her, he went on, 'Perhaps it will help to convince you if I tell you that my love for you has been driving me out of my mind. That after that time in Wales when I thought you thoroughly detested me, I had to take myself off abroad in case I was weak enough to come looking for you again. That when I saw you at the office this morning I had to fight with everything I knew not to weaken, fight like hell not to lose all the strength I'd been storing up against you this past couple of weeks.'

'Is that—that why you looked as though you hated me?' she asked, too afraid yet to really believe this wonderful thing was happening to her.

'I could never hate you,' he said gently. 'But for the sake of my sanity I didn't want to see you again. Though I think I held sanity by the merest whisker when I saw your cheque, and insane jealousy took me over.' He lowered his head and kissed her wonder-parted lips. 'I love you, dearest Aldona,' he said softly. 'Are you going to be brave and confess what I'm longing to hear?'

Shock at the miracle of what he was saying was holding her speechless, and it was left to Zeb to entice the confession he wanted to hear from her, as he said, not a smile in evidence:

'I don't mind telling you I felt as though my world had ended when I thought at the cottage that you loathed me.'

'Oh, Zeb,' she rushed in, unable to bear as he had hoped, the thought of his sufferings that night, 'I love you so!'

A smile broke from him that was wonderful to see, and without waiting for her to say any more, he scooped her up in his arms and kissed her in a way that left her in no doubt as to the strength of his feelings.

'My darling love,' he said, breaking his kiss and gazing into her eyes as though it was some miracle for him too. 'And to think I tried for weeks to deny that I loved you.'

'You did?' she questioned in a whisper.

'Without much success,' he smiled, planting delicate kisses about her ear, his lips moving back to hers. 'In Malta I tried to convince myself I was only taking you from Downs to spoil at least one of his extra-marital activities. I told myself when you ran out on me there that it didn't bother me. It wasn't my intention to come looking for you, but before I knew what I was doing, I was doing just that.'

'I'm glad you did,' she said softly, and was kissed again, and asking when Zeb's mouth left hers and he leaned back to look at her as if he could quite happily sit there for hours doing just that, when had he finally acknowledged that he loved her.

'At the cottage,' he said, a wry smile crossing his face, 'I had to face up to it when I found myself actually making up a bed in the spare room.' His grin broadened and he gave her a wicked look. 'Believe me, that hadn't been my intention at all.' His face returned to being serious when he told her, 'It was then I had to face up to what this feeling was that kept me awake nights thinking about you.'

'Oh, darling!' sighed Aldona, the word leaving her shyly.

Then all was quiet as Zeb began an assault on her senses that had her mindless of anything but her need for him. Then just when she thought he would take her past the barrier and into that enchanting world that promised, his lips left hers. And with his arms still round her as if he was loath to let her go, he sat up, taking her with him, his eyes dark with emotion as he searched her face.

'You are going to marry me, aren't you?' he asked, and she heard the touch of aggressiveness in his question that had her thinking with astonishment that for a man who had always shown himself so much in command, so sure of himself, unbelievably, when she thought she had clearly shown what her answer would be, he didn't appear to be very sure at all.

'Oh yes, Zeb,' she answered, wondering if her heart would ever beat normally again. 'If that's what you want.'

'If that's what I want!' he echoed, looking affronted. 'I'll settle for nothing less.' Then, 'What's the matter?' that aggressiveness there again. 'Aren't you sure?'

'Yes, yes. Oh Zeb, yes, I'm sure. It's just that I'm so confused at the moment—finding you love me, asking me to marry you, when I haven't explained yet anything of what I was doing—in Malta.'

'I don't need to know anything about what you were doing in Malta, all I need to know is that you love me. If you want a fur coat I'll give you a hundred, but you've got to love me, got to marry me.'

'Zeb, Zeb, I do, I will—you've no idea of the agonies I've been through wanting you to love me, but thinking you never could, never would—and ... and I never, ever want a wretched fur coat!'

Zeb needed no persuading at this point to take her in his arms, and in a long and totally loving kiss, he blotted all the agonies she had ever suffered from her mind. But when he drew back from her, still holding her as though he wasn't easily going to let her go and thoroughly enjoyed having her there in the shelter of his arms, Aldona knew she had to tell him all there was to tell him, to tell him now, to get it all said and over with for ever.

'Zeb—about Malta.' The seriousness of her expression told him she had to tell him and his arms tightened protectively about her as though to say whatever pain there was to be for either of them in what she had to say, then nothing was going to hurt the love they shared. But when she began to speak, to tell him about Lionel Downs' treachery, how she had been terrified her father would die if she didn't go with him, there came about Zeb such a violence of expression that Aldona found it was she who was holding strongly on to him, fearful he would get up and leave her to find Lionel and do him some injury that would permanently maim him or worse.

'It's all over now,' she said, hanging grimly on to him, not sure yet that he wouldn't storm away from her in search of his soon to be *ex*-stepfather. 'And anyway,' she added, trying for a light note, 'if I hadn't gone to Malta, we would never have met.'

With relief, she saw that had brought Zeb back to her quicker than anything else she could have said. 'My darling,' he said, his dark grey eyes burning into hers, his voice thick with emotion. 'Oh, my darling, darling girl! To think you've been through all that, all the mental anguish and suffering you've been through—some of it at my hands too . . .' He broke off as though his thoughts were too much for him to take. Then with a gentleness that was almost a benediction, he tenderly kissed her eyes, transferring his warm mouth to her lips. 'I shall make it all up to you,' he said. 'Never again will you know such terrible anxiety.'

His words were said as a vow, and deeply stirred, Aldona clutched convulsively on his shoulders. All that was in the past. The future promised to be wonderful.

'I love you, Zeb,' she said softly, just before his lips met hers.

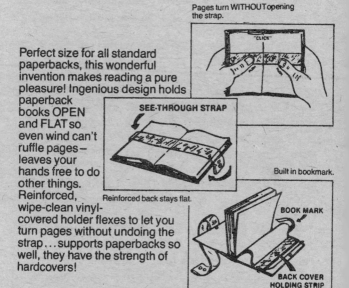